D0756722

HIGHLAND WOLF

ALSO BY ALICIA MONTGOMERY

Highland Wolf

Daughter of the Dragon

Shadow Wolf

A Touch of Magic

Heart of the Wolf

THE BLACKSTONE MOUNTAIN SERIES

The Blackstone Dragon Heir

The Blackstone Bad Dragon

The Blackstone Bear

The Blackstone Wolf

The Blackstone Lion

The Blackstone She-Wolf

The Blackstone She-Bear

The Blackstone She-Dragon

This is a work of fiction. Names, characters, businesses, places, events, locales, and incidents are either the products of the author's imagination or used in a fictitious manner. Any resemblance to actual persons, living or dead, or actual events is purely coincidental.

COPYRIGHT © 2019 ALICIA MONTGOMERY
EDITED BY LAVERNE CLARK
COVER BY JACQUELINE SWEET

ALL RIGHTS RESERVED.

HIGHLAND WOLF

TRUE MATES GENERATIONS BOOK 5

ALICIA MONTGOMERY

CHAPTER ONE

JULIANNA ANDERSON WIPED THE BLOOD FROM HER mouth with the back of her hand. "That was a lucky shot."

Her opponent, Chase Harris, shot her a flirtatious grin, his blue eyes sparkling. "So you say."

Anger simmered to the surface, and her wolf begged to be let out. *No*, she told the she-wolf. *This is an exercise for humans.* As a member of the Lycan Security Team for New York, she had to hone both her human and wolf side. For the last six years, she'd been assigned to the special investigations division that watched over the clan and its members.

In the last couple of months, however, she'd taken on a new role. When her sister, Adrianna, ascended to Alpha of New Jersey, she'd needed help training her own security team, and Julianna had volunteered right away.

"You are not concentrating." Her brother-in-law, Darius Corvinus, stood behind her, his voice soft so only she could hear him. Not only was he her sister's mate and husband, but he also was her co-trainer.

"Not with you yappin' in my ear like that, Darius." She

gritted her teeth then waved a wrapped hand at Chase. "C'mon, pretty boy, try again."

"Aww, you think I'm pretty, Anderson?" He shot her another panty-melting smile. Well, maybe any other girls' panties would have melted, but not Julianna's. No, he'd already tried to charm his way into her bed, and while it was tempting, she didn't shit where she ate.

"Suck my dick, Harris."

"You know, for a girl, you sure do tell people to suck your dick a lot."

"Are you guys gonna fight or what?" Angela Hall, one of the other trainees, said with a bored expression as she tossed her cornrow braids over her shoulder.

Julianna liked the spunky young she-wolf, as she reminded her a lot of herself when she began training. "You know Harris. All talk, no action. Hey!" No sooner than the yelp escaped her mouth, she found herself flat on her back with Chase hovering over her. Recovering quickly though, she swept a leg under him, sending him crashing down to the ground. Her wolf howled in triumph. "That was a dirty move."

"Yeah, well our enemies aren't always going to fight fair." Chase got up, then offered her a hand.

Fucking hell, she hated to admit it, but he was right. Refusing his hand, she stood up on her own.

"Everything okay here?"

All at once, the trainees stood up straight and turned to the source of the voice. Julianna brushed the blades of grass stuck to her yoga pants and then smirked up at her sister, who was descending the porch steps of the old Victorian mansion. Only Adrianna Anderson could look regal while eight months pregnant. Darius immediately rushed to her side to hold her hand.

"For God's sake, Darius, I'm pregnant, not an invalid," she said, her tone annoyed.

"You should not be up and about," he scolded.

"Have you forgotten that nothing can harm me?" Since she was pregnant with her True Mate's child, Adrianna was invincible. No one knew why, exactly, but that was just the way it was.

"Yes, I know." Darius sighed. "But a fall could still hurt you. And I do not want you in pain."

"I know, but nothing's going to happen to me." She smiled up warmly at him, then turned to the recruits. "Good morning, everyone," she greeted. "I trust that training is going well."

"Yes, Primul," they all said in unison, using the traditional honorific Lycans called their Alpha.

"Good." She turned to Julianna and winced. "Did you hurt yourself?"

She covered the cut above her lip with her hand. "It'll be good in a few hours."

"How about a break?" Adrianna cocked her head toward the house. "You guys have been at it since dawn."

The training was tough, but it had to be. There was so much more at stake, now that the mages, their archenemies, had resurfaced after thirty years and then attacked them repeatedly. Julianna's wolf growled at the thought of those evil bastards and what they did. It was only the thought of stopping them once and for all that kept her going these days, especially when she was reminded of the events of the past. *No, don't think of it. Don't think of that. Don't think of* them.

"Julianna?" Her sister's look was that of concern. "Are you—"

"I'm great," she said. "We don't need a break."

The collective groans from the trainees made her whip her head back and narrow her eyes at them.

Adrianna placed her hands on her hips. "In that case, I'm ordering you to take a break."

She very well couldn't ignore a direct order from her Alpha. Well, Adrianna technically wasn't *her* Alpha since Julianna was born into the New York clan. Their father, Grant Anderson, had been the Alpha then, and she'd always been part of his clan. But their mother was also Alpha of New Jersey before Adrianna, and Julianna was now helping Adrianna so, well, frankly, she didn't know where she belonged. *Not anymore.*

Squashing those dark thoughts threatening to weigh her down, she pivoted to the house. "Fine. Let's go inside." As she followed Adrianna and Darius, she winced. "Jesus, how can you move? You look like you should have given birth yesterday."

Adrianna laughed, her mismatched eyes—one blue and one green—sparkled. "I manage. I imagine when you get pregnant, you'll carry it better. Taller women always do." While she and all her siblings inherited the heterochromia from their mother, Adrianna and their youngest sister also got their petite stature from her. Julianna was tall and athletic like her brother and father.

"Highly unlikely, since I don't plan on ever getting pregnant," she snorted.

Adrianna raised a brow, but said nothing, and instead motioned for her to take a seat at the kitchen table. Her sister then poured some coffee from the pot, sat beside her and then pushed the cup toward her. "Julianna, Darius told me that you've been ... off, lately."

"Off?" It was hard not to sound defensive because the comment caught her off guard. *How did he—*

"You are distracted," Darius said. "And unfocused."

Her nostrils flared, and she narrowed her eyes at him. Even her wolf seemed offended by the implication that she was not competent.

Once upon a time, she truly hated Darius's guts, but that changed when he nearly died to save all of them from the mages. He also showed them all that he truly loved Adrianna. Julianna was now his biggest fan and co-conspirator, especially when it came to protecting Adrianna. Her sister would often joke that she didn't know if she preferred them to be enemies or friends, especially when they fussed over her.

Right this moment, however, she really wanted to claw his eyes out. "I don't know what you mean."

Adrianna's eyes dropped to the cut on her lip and Julianna instinctively shielded it by lifting the coffee cup to her mouth. The damn liquid was hot and burned her throat as she swallowed, but she didn't dare show them any sign of weakness.

"Julianna." Adrianna reached over to put a hand on her shoulder. "Do you need to talk about something? Ever since what happened at Lucas's ascension ceremony ..."

The deep melancholy was there again, creeping in, but she wouldn't let it take over. *Never.* Her wolf growled as that heavy feeling was present enough for the animal to feel it. The bottom of the coffee cup met the table with such force that it cracked the porcelain. "Shit!" She rushed toward the sink, tossing the cup as hot brown liquid seeped from the fracture. "Sorry. I'll fix that." She took a deep breath but didn't dare turn around to face them. How could she, when they could see right through her?

"Adrianna? Darius? Are you home?"

Spinning around, her eyes immediately tracked toward the newcomer standing in the kitchen doorway. She had been so distracted she didn't even hear him arrive.

"Lucas, you're early." Adrianna got to her feet, but before she could even take one step, her twin brother quickly crossed the room and accepted her hug, then motioned for her to sit down. "For crying out loud, not you too."

He put up his hands defensively. "Hey, Sofia's a month behind you, but she's already cranky if she has to get up and grab the TV remote."

"How is Sofia these days?" Adrianna asked.

"She's healthy." He frowned. "But if her captain didn't force her to take maternity leave, you know she'd be chasing down suspects until her water broke."

Julianna guffawed. Her NYPD detective sister-in-law was tough, and she could totally see her doing that, which is why she respected Sofia so much.

"Hey, Julianna," Lucas greeted as he came over to the sink. "How's—" He frowned when his gaze dropped to her swollen lip. "What happened?"

"Training," she said with a shrug. "What're you doing here?" Adrianna seemed to have expected him, but Julianna certainly didn't know he was coming by to visit.

Before he could answer, a loud, frustrated sigh drifted into the kitchen. "Ugh! Why hasn't the cellphone company fixed the signal around here? I've been trying to post this photo since we got off the highway!"

Julianna stiffened as she heard the voice of her youngest sister. Sure enough, Isabelle Anderson strutted into the kitchen like she was on a catwalk at Fashion Week, dressed head to toe in designer clothes. "You know, the world won't stop revolving if you don't post photos to your social media pages every ten seconds."

Isabelle flipped her long, glossy hair over her shoulder. "This is my job, Julianna. People expect to be updated on the latest trends and fashion."

"Job?" she sneered. "Right. Being a walking talking billboard—"

"Okay, *children*." Lucas massaged the bridge on his nose. "Stop before I make you both stand in the corner."

"She started it!" wailed Isabelle.

"Did not!" Julianna stuck her tongue out at her.

"I don't care who started it, I'm going to end it." He shook his head and rubbed a hand down his face. "Why do I always sound like Mom around you two?"

Adrianna cleared her throat. "Isabelle, why don't you come upstairs with me? That's why you're here, right, to help me with the nursery?" Getting up from her seat, she made her way to the younger woman and linked their arms.

"I have so many ideas!" Isabelle clapped her hands, seemingly forgetting about Julianna. "I saw the cutest bassinet at. ..." She trailed off as they walked out the kitchen, but not before Adrianna signaled to her husband, who followed them.

"Can you guys ever be in the same room without starting a fight?" Lucas said in an irritated voice.

It's not that she hated Isabelle; she was family for God's sake, and she loved her youngest sister. But they were as different as night and day. Isabelle was vain and vapid and never took anything seriously. Julianna, on the other hand, was single-minded and focused.

"She was the one who—" When Lucas gave her a warning look, she scowled. "I get it. She's your favorite. You and Papa both."

His jaw hardened. "Julianna, that's just not true."

She crossed her arms over her chest. "Isn't it?"

"Look," he began, his tone gentle. "No one is mine or Papa's favorite. But Isabelle ... can't you see? She's always needed a little more help and attention. You, on the other hand, you've never needed our help. Remember when you had that science fair and Mama forgot to help you because she was stuck in Chicago during that snowstorm? When she got home, she was so apologetic, and what did you do?"

The corner of her mouth tugged up involuntarily. "I showed her the volcano I made from the stuff I found around the house."

His face lit up. "See? You never complained, never got mad, didn't even cry. Instead, you pulled yourself up by your bootstraps and got things done." He put a hand on her shoulder. "You've always been independent and wise beyond your years. Which is why I came here."

She shot him a confused look. "You came here because of me?"

"Yes." He motioned for her to sit at the table.

She took the seat she'd previously occupied. "What's this about?" Lucas's demeanor had changed, as she often observed he did when it was a matter of clan business. The man standing before her now wasn't just her older brother, but also, the Alpha of the most powerful clan in the world.

"As you know, the mages haven't resurfaced in the past couple of months. Not since my ascension ceremony."

As if by sheer willpower alone, she stopped the cold sweat threatening to form on her temples at the mention of that particular event. "I don't think they've given up."

"Not by a long shot."

"And the third artifact?" The mages were trying to collect three artifacts that once belonged to a powerful mage, Magus Aurelius. It was said that when all three were brought together, the mages would gain magic and power that no one had ever seen in a thousand years. No one was sure what that power would be like exactly, but if the mages wanted them bad enough, then it had something to do with killing all the Lycans in the world and enslaving humanity. As of the moment, the mages had one of the artifacts, while the Lycans had another. The third was still a mystery.

"No leads," he said. "Cross has been searching for months." Cross Jonasson was a hybrid—half wolf and half warlock—who could travel long distances and bend matter to his will. He had been tasked with finding all of the artifacts before the mages did.

"What can I do to help, then?" Just thinking about the artifacts made her nauseous. But, if Lucas needed her, she wasn't going to back down. But how could she even begin any search for the artifacts? Where would she look?

"I want you to be my envoy," Lucas said. "And meet with other Alphas to begin forming alliances." Although Lycan clans all over the world were loosely connected and governed by a central body—the Lycan High Council—they didn't have any formal connections or partnerships, unless it was through marriage. Even then, there was no agreement that one clan would come in aid of another. Not that the clans didn't get along, but in these modern times, wars or being exposed to humans simply weren't as big an issue as it had been before, so alliances were no longer a necessity.

"Lucas, I'm not exactly the diplomatic type." Indeed, she was the *opposite* of diplomatic. "Why not send someone else? Someone who's a people person. Like Jared or Aunt Cady?"

"They can't, they're needed here. Don't underestimate yourself, Julianna. You can be very persuasive if you want to be," he said. "Besides, all you have to do is meet with the Alphas as my official representative and get the ball rolling. I'll take care of closing the deal. I don't like the idea of sending you out when the mages could attack at any time, but I know you've trained well as part of the Lycan Security Force and can handle yourself."

She chewed on her lip. "But what about Adrianna and Darius? They need me too."

"I've talked it over with them, and they said that they're willing to spare you if you want to go. Think of it as a chance to travel and see new things at the very least. I mean, c'mon, Julianna, I can't ask anyone else." He took her hand. "Papa and I can't *trust* anyone else."

His words totally gobsmacked her. True, Lucas and Papa never coddled or indulged her, and now she realized that was because they knew she was capable. Frankly, that meant a whole lot more to her than having them taking her side in a petty argument with Isabelle. Her wolf practically preened at the praise from its Alpha. "Of course." She nodded resolutely. "I'm here. Whatever you need."

"Good." He took something out of his pocket—a small velvet box. Opening it, he presented her with a necklace. The chain was thin, made of gold, and there was a small medallion at the end. There was a face of a wolf on the front and in the back, a strange-looking seal with a tree, a crowned red wolf, and vines on a field of green and silver. "Cross found that seal in his research. He says it's the original New York clan coat of arms. We haven't needed to use it in decades, but I thought this would be appropriate." He paused. "He also infused it with magic so that the chain grows when you shift so you don't have to worry about destroying it."

She wrinkled her nose at the medal. "But what is it?"

"Just a small token to signify that you're my envoy," he said. "Some clans still recognize the symbol, so I thought I'd have it made for you."

She took the necklace and put it over her head, then tucked it into her shirt, the gold warming against her skin. "When do I start?"

Lucas smiled at her. "I'd like you to leave in a few days. And, since I wanted to make it easier on you, I thought I'd have some people to go along with you on your first two destinations."

"Great," she said. "Who and where?"

"Elise and Reed. You're going to Scotland first and then England. They're headed there for a delayed honeymoon of sorts. Elise told me she and Reed have been wanting to go back to pay their respects. I thought it would make sense and you all could go along."

The cold sweat finally did break out on her forehead and the back of her neck. *Goddammit*. And from the look on Lucas's face, it seemed like he thought it was the best and most logical idea ever. She swallowed. Unfortunately, there was no way she could back out now. Not when Lucas and Papa put so much faith in her. "Great," she croaked. "When do I leave?"

––––––

When she first called Elise to ask her if she could join their trip, Julianna had hoped she would say no.

"Of course you can come," Elise had said enthusiastically. "I haven't seen you since ... well ... I guess since that night we came back. How have you been?"

That night we came back. Elise made it sound like they had gone on vacation or something. "Good. Fine. Yeah, been busy. Helping train Adrianna's wolves. So ... you *don't* mind if I come along?"

"Not at all. It's been ages. Besides, alliances with other Alphas? That sounds like a good idea."

It's not that she didn't want to see her. In the short time she and Elise spent together, she grew to like the hybrid who could shoot electricity from her fingers. No, the problem was she and her mate, Reed, reminded her of that event she just wanted to put behind her and forget altogether.

Event was perhaps too mild a word for what happened, which was that she, Elise, and Cross had been transported to the year 1820 by one of the artifacts of Magus Aurelius.

The three of them spent two weeks in Regency England, though when they returned, only a few minutes had passed for everyone else. Also, much to their surprise, Reed Townsend turned out to be Elise's True Mate and had been transported back to the future with them, though he had arrived three months before and had been waiting for her return all that time.

Everyone celebrated and welcomed them back, of course. They were amazed by their stories, and of course, amused by Reed's impressions of the future. And it was a good thing, because they were distracted and didn't notice Julianna pull away from them.

And that's when it began.

Some days she would have dreams of the past that were so real, she woke up in a cold sweat. Other times, something would trigger her memory, like a commercial for a period film or passing by an antiques store. And worse was when it would just pop out of nowhere and she felt it: a realization that everything and everyone she got to know those two weeks were gone. Eleanor. Jeremy. Bridget. The dowager. Yes, even little William, Reed's young nephew. All dead. Turned to dust by now.

"Ms. Anderson?"

The driver's voice jolted her out of her thoughts, though that heaviness still weighed on her chest. That's right, she was here, now. In the present. Waiting at the private airstrip so she could start their journey. She placed her hand over her chest, feeling for the small, gold disc that hung from the chain around her neck. Lucas was counting on her. "Yes?"

"They're here."

Peering out of the SUV, she saw the limo pulling into the tarmac. She knew who was coming to the private airstrip, so she didn't even bother to wait as she pulled on the door to open it. When she saw them exit the limo, her heart burst, realizing how much she missed them. "Elise! Reed!"

They both looked at her, their smiles warm. Elise and

Reed now lived in San Francisco, as she was the Alpha's daughter and he pledged to their clan. They flew commercial to New York and now they would all fly together to Scotland. The use of the plane for their trip there, to London, and back to New York was a delayed gift from Julianna's father, Grant Anderson, former Alpha of New York.

Before they could say anything, she pulled Elise into a tight hug. "It's so nice to see you. Oops!" She stepped back when she felt the bump poking at her stomach. "Hey, momma, you've popped!" It was obvious that pregnancy hadn't had any bad effects as Elise had the gorgeous glow of happiness.

"She has, and she's beautiful," said Reed in that elegant posh accent of his. "How are you, Julianna?"

Pasting a smile on her face, she said, "I'm great."

"I see you haven't cut your hair as you threatened a million times," he noted.

Doing a perfect imitation of Isabelle, she grabbed her braid and flipped it over her shoulder. "It's growing on me." Julianna had always worn her hair short as it was easier to maintain. When they had been transported back to the 1800s, Cross had used his magic to grow it out so she could fit in. When they came back, she was ready to cut it, but part of her just ... *couldn't*. Whenever she took a pair of scissors to it, flashes of Jane—the maid who was assigned to help her dress and get ready each day—came back to her. The young woman had been so sweet and so talented at styling hair. She'd always complimented Julianna and told her how she envied her long, thick black hair.

But Jane was gone. Just like everyone else.

She cleared her throat and pushed those thoughts away. "Thanks again for letting me horn in on your babymoon."

"Babymoon?" Reed asked.

"You know." She pointed her chin at Elise's bump. "Last chance to get some alone time before the baby comes."

"Ha! My parents and siblings are so excited and preparing to come visit us all the time that I doubt we'd even have time with the baby when he or she comes." Elise glanced up at the waiting plane. "Should we get going? We want to get there by morning, right?"

They all boarded the plane and settled themselves into the plush leather seats as the steward offered them champagne and juice. Soon, they were soaring over the clouds and would be comfortably cruising for the next seven hours or so to Glasgow. It was late, and so the steward served dinner not too long after takeoff.

"Traveling takes a lot outta me." Elise let out a long, loud yawn after they finished eating. "Well, almost anything takes a lot out of me these days."

"You should get some rest, love." Reed placed a hand on her belly.

"There's a private room with a bed," Julianna said, pointing toward the rear of the plane. "Go ahead and use it."

"How about you?"

"I don't really need to sleep, plus I have to catch up on some work. And these"—she motioned to the chairs—"turn into lie-flat beds. No, don't worry, they're comfortable. Much more comfy than all of us trying to fit into that double bed in the back."

Elise looked like she had no strength to protest, so Reed got up with her and helped her to the bedroom.

Since they had a couple more hours to go, Julianna took out her laptop, trying to concentrate on the files Jared had sent her about the first Alpha she was to going to meet. Callum MacDougal was in his sixties and had been Alpha of Caelkirk for the last twenty-five years. He had a Lupa, Kirsten, and six children.

"What are you doing?" Reed asked when he came back into the main cabin.

"Just reading up on our hosts."

He sat down on the chair opposite hers. "Anything interesting?" She turned the screen to face him and his brow furrowed. "Oh, I've read the same file from the Lycan High Council, I think. Did you also get Cross's research?"

"I don't think so." She scrolled to the end of the report. Really, it was all boring and dry facts.

"Since he was doing research on the artifacts, he went ahead and looked up what happened to the London and Caelkirk clans after ... I disappeared."

For a second, she saw his composure slip. While she had only known those people from the past for two weeks, Reed had known them his whole life. Surely whatever she felt was magnified ten times for him.

"Since you didn't get Cross's research, I think you'd be happy to know that Bridget found her True Mate."

"Oh." Bridget MacDonald was Reed's Scottish cousin who came to London the same time they did, searching for her True Mate. "She mentioned something about meeting him the night of your ball. Who was he?"

"His name was Connor MacDougal, and I actually met him." There was a fond smile on his face.

"Huh." She leaned forward. "Who was he? Was he nice? Good enough for her?"

He chuckled. "I only met him that day for a few hours, and we mostly talked about how to defend ourselves from the mages. He's her True Mate, so you can be assured he was good to her."

Of course he was. Julianna had seen it all her life—how True Mates acted around each other. Her mother and father, for example, adored each other, and it was obvious there was nothing either wouldn't do to make the other happy.

And she really was happy for Bridget. There were times when she couldn't sleep at night, when the weight pressed on her chest so bad, she couldn't breathe, that she liked to think that everyone from back then had gone on to live fulfilling lives.

"You know, it's all right to miss them. All of them. Eleanor. Grandmama. Jeremy and William."

Her head snapped toward him, and she realized that this was the first time since she came back that she'd heard their names spoken out loud. She hadn't dared; couldn't, fearing her chest would be crushed with the weight of the reality of them being gone. "I—" The tears burned at her throat, making it hard to speak.

"It's all right." His tone was so gentle, like a warm fuzzy blanket over her. "What you went through ... I imagine no one else can relate. At least Elise has me and I have her. I'm sure you're not close enough to Cross to confide in him."

True. Though they had gone through that event together, it wasn't like she and Cross were immediately BFFs now. Heck, she hadn't even seen him at all since that night.

"Do you know, I thought all three of you were complete

lunatics that morning you first came to Hunter House?" Reed's mouth was quirked into a smile.

The chuckle escaped her throat at the memory. "Cross had to go find us some clothes to wear, and he didn't realize he stole ballgowns."

"I thought your manners were atrocious." He shook his head. "I hope you'll forgive me for being insufferable the entire time."

"Meh, there's nothing to forgive." She waved a hand. "You were a product of your time and upbringing. And we were these weirdos who came out of nowhere."

As the hours wore on, Reed spoke more about his family, the past, and of course, his impressions on being in the future. Julianna found it all fascinating, especially when he spoke about encountering things like computers and cars. They had never really sat down and spoken at length before, and she had to admit, though her first impression of him hadn't been great, she could see he was a man of integrity and had a big heart.

"The only thing I'm disappointed in is that over two hundred years later, prejudice still hasn't been eradicated." He frowned. "Why should it matter what—"

"Excuse me, Ms. Anderson, Mr. Wakefield." The steward stepped out of the galley. "We'll be landing in about an hour. If you'd like to freshen up, I can serve breakfast any time before then."

"Oh dear, where did the time go?" He tsked at his watch. "I'll go see if Elise wants to eat. Actually, I know she'll want to eat."

"Me too," Julianna said.

The steward nodded. "I'll get the food ready then."

"Thank you." With one last smile at Julianna, Reed left to go back to the bedroom.

Julianna headed to the washroom so she could do her business and splash water on her face. When she came out, Elise and Reed were already seated. After the quick breakfast, the plane landed in Glasgow Airport. From there, it was a four-hour drive to Caelkirk in their rented SUV. Since Reed didn't know how to operate a car and Elise would be uncomfortable driving for such a long period of time, Julianna volunteered to drive.

"I can see why your mother loved it here. It's beautiful," Elise remarked as she popped her head between the front seats.

Julianna had to agree. The Scottish landscapes were beautiful. "Did you visit here a lot?"

"I've only been three times," Reed said. "Twice when I was younger and then ..."

"I'm sure you had a lovely time," Elise finished.

He let out a guffaw. "Yes, I did, if you define 'lovely time' as being plagued by pranks from my mother's relatives for being a 'Sassenach.'" But there was a fond smile that touched his lips.

She slowed the vehicle when she saw their exit approaching. "So, are we going to stay with the clan?"

Elise nodded. "Dad took care of everything and contacted the clan on our behalf."

"He told their Alpha the story of me being adopted and never knowing my true nature until I met Elise," Reed continued. "And that I was probably from the Caelkirk or London clan and wanted to research my roots."

It was too dangerous to let everyone know where Reed

really came from, so they concocted a believable story to explain how he just suddenly appeared. Everyone who knew about it agreed it was better to keep it a secret, just in case the mages realized how powerful the dagger truly was.

"The Alpha agreed to host us at Castle Kilcraigh and allow us to tour the grounds," he continued. "According to Cross's research, he's Bridget's direct descendant."

"I'm really glad Bridget met her mate," Julianna said. "And you said that Connor guy was okay?"

"I only met him for a moment," Reed confessed. "But he seemed a decent sort to me." As they drove past a moss-covered wall, he announced, "We're here. Look."

Julianna whistled. "Wow."

When Lucas told her that they'd been invited to stay at Castle Kilcraigh, she didn't think it was a *literal* castle, complete with a moat, stone walls, turrets, and spikes. She quickly turned her eyes back to the road and pulled into the front. When she parked the car, they gathered their things and began to walk toward the entrance.

A man in a tweed suit was waiting for them by the door.

"You must be our guests from America. I'm Gerald MacDougal, Beta of the Caelkirk clan." The Scottish brogue was a bit difficult to understand, but his tone was welcoming. The Beta had a warm smile and reminded Julianna of a friendly uncle. However, because of her training with the Lycan Security Team, she couldn't help but sense the presence of his wolf which seemed wary of the three strangers.

"Thank you for welcoming us and allowing us into the territory," Reed greeted back. "I'm Reed Wakefield, this is my wife, Elise, daughter to Liam Henney, Alpha of San Francisco, and Julianna Anderson, envoy and sister to Lucas Anderson, Alpha of New York."

"Thank you for welcoming us," Elise said.

"Nice to meet you all," he said as he shook hands with Reed, then did the same with Elise. When he turned to Julianna, his took her offered hand, but didn't let go. His bushy brows drew together. "Do I know you?"

"I don't think so." There was no sexual interest or malice in his tone, only genuine confusion. "Have you ever been to New York?"

"No, but it's like ... I could have sworn ..." He scratched at his chin. "It's like I've seen you before." Letting go of her hand, he shook his head. "I'm sorry my Alpha's not here to greet you. He and his son had a sudden meeting in town, and he's not sure when they'll be back. But, don't you worry, we're all ready for you." He nodded to the older woman walking toward them. "Mrs. Carter, she's the housekeeper around here, will have your things sent up to your rooms. Unfortunately, I'm about to pop into a conference call myself, but please feel free to look around the grounds. I'll be out around two, and we can take a tour of the castle after we have tea."

"Excellent idea," Reed said. "I would like to go for a walk."

"I'll join you. It'll give me a chance to stretch my legs." Elise slipped her arm through Reed's.

"I'm pooped." She *had* been awake for seven hours and drove for another four hours. Anyone would be tired, even a Lycan. "If you wouldn't mind, I need a shower and a nap, but that tea and tour sounds great."

"It's all settled then," Gerald clapped his hands together.

"Julianna, you can follow Mrs. Carter, and we can all meet here at two."

"Come right this way, Ms. Julianna." Mrs. Carter was already headed toward the grand staircase. "I'll show you to your room."

"Thank you." She followed the older woman and climbed the staircase. On the landing, they passed a magnificent stained glass window before turning right toward the east wing. For a moment, she hesitated. It was obvious that although the outside and the roads had been modernized, all the interiors and furniture were antiques. She was afraid that being here would remind her of the past and bring back that heavy, dark feeling. To her surprise, it didn't. Maybe it was because this wasn't Huntington Park or Hunter House, or anywhere she'd been before in 1820.

Her wolf, too, was acting curiously. It was sniffing with its head in the air, trying to catch a scent. When she breathed in, she took in a faint scent of malt, pine, and earth.

"Here ya go," Mrs. Carter said cheerfully as they entered the bedroom. "Hope it's to your liking, miss?"

To her relief, the bedroom was nothing like the rooms she stayed in back in 1820. The bedrooms in Eleanor's home, Hunter House, and Huntington Park were all sumptuous and elegant. This room was cozy and had a more rugged and masculine feel, decorated in rich mahoganies and reds. A tartan bedspread covered the enormous four-poster bed. "It's wonderful. Thank you."

"I'll leave you to get refreshed, but if there's anything you need, just give us a ring." She nodded to the intercom on the bedside table.

"Thank you, Mrs. Carter."

As soon as she was alone, she unpacked, took a shower and went down for a short nap. Her alarm went off at exactly one thirty. She decided to leave her hair down, and after getting dressed in a sweater, leggings, and knee-high boots, made her way downstairs to the foyer. Gerald was already there, and once again, he was looking at her curiously. Before he could say anything, Elise and Reed came in through the front door.

Gerald turned to them. "Did you have a nice walk?"

"We did."

"Good. We can start in the library where I have tea set up." The Beta led them down the hallway on the right. "Here we go." He opened the last door and led them in toward a sitting area by the fireplace. Julianna's stomach growled at the smell of fresh pastries and tea.

"Let's—oh." Gerald stopped in his tracks, looked at the fireplace and then at Julianna. "I thought I had ... but how ...?"

With her thoughts totally on the scones, jam and—*holy shit*—real clotted cream on the table, she didn't even notice everyone staring at her.

"Oh." Elise's mouth was open. "Oh my."

Frowning, she followed her gaze.

Holy. Fucking. Moly.

Her gut twisted as a dark, heavy feeling began to seep into her, right down to her bones. *The painting.* More specifically, *her portrait.*

Back in 1820, the London clan had a guest from Italy— Signore Rossi, an envoy for the Prince of Florence. He also happened to be an artist and had begged to paint her portrait. Julianna sat for it, seeing as she didn't really have a choice back then. She recalled all the hours she'd spent sitting still for Rossi, and the way his eyes sparkled as he exalted her beauty and features, to the point of being uncomfortable.

It wasn't that she thought Rossi had wanted to sleep with her or anything—no, Rossi had seemed more like an adoring grandpa. She'd been uncomfortable because she never saw herself as beautiful. She knew that her face was too angular, and compared to her mother and sisters, she was almost masculine. A plain Jane. And maybe that's why she always strove to excel in other ways.

But—oh—this painting. Was that really her? It looked like her, but ... it was like a completely different person. This person was beautiful and sensual, and something in her smile and eyes was almost mysterious.

"Are you all right?"

Elise's voice snapped her out of her reverie. "I'm great. Dandy." *Deep breaths. Take deep breaths.* "I should—I need— I'm—" Spinning around, she dashed toward the door like it was her motherfucking salvation. However, before she could cross the threshold, she bumped into something very solid. *Fuck!*

"Whoa!" Her body was falling back, but a pair of strong arms wrapped around her. Her knees, however, went weak. Her wolf froze, but as soon as the scent hit its nose—peat, malt, and pine—just like the faint smell she detected earlier— it went crazy, rolling around the ground and yowling. "I—" Another deep breath. But it was no use, because when she looked up and saw a pair of bright green eyes, all the air rushed out of her lungs.

"It's you," he said. "It's really you."

CHAPTER TWO

———————

Duncan MacDougal remembered the exact moment he first saw the painting.

He was seven years old, visiting the London Alpha's country estate, Huntington Park. The London and Caerlkirk clans had been close allies for generations, having been related by marriage at one point. Seeing as he would be Alpha one day, his father, Callum MacDougal, thought it was time for Duncan to meet their allies. So, he brought his mate Kirsten, and his growing brood to London to meet John Griffiths, Duke of Huntington and Alpha of London.

The Alpha had a grandson, Oliver, who was only a year older than Duncan. As boys of their age did, they went around Huntington Park, exploring all the rooms and nooks and crannies of the old estate. They had been going around for what seemed like hours when they came upon what must have been a storage room. Old furniture, boxes, and broken-down appliances littered the dank and dusty room, and the only light came from a single window in the back.

Oliver had dared him to go in alone, and, not wanting to appear weak to his new playmate, Duncan did it despite the chills going down his spine. He remembered wishing he had his wolf, but alas, Lycans only first shifted during puberty. The roar of his blood in his ears and the pounding of his heart in his little chest was something he would never forget.

Deeper he went, tiptoeing through the cramped spaces, until he reached the back. The only window in the room allowed some sun inside, and a shaft of light hit a large, square object covered by a cloth.

There was something that compelled Duncan to grab the cloth and pull it away. To this day, he wasn't sure what, but he could remember that exact moment, when, as the dusty fabric dropped to the floor, it revealed *her*.

The woman in the painting was pretty, he supposed, but being only seven years old he wasn't quite at that age to say for sure. But he could clearly remember those eyes. One green and one blue. How peculiar. And that dark hair flowing down her shoulders, that mysterious smile. It seemed like an old painting, but whoever made it didn't finish it, based on the unpainted portion of the canvas. Why?

Oliver had called him from outside the room, and, fearing that he had done something he wasn't supposed to, quickly covered up the painting and ran outside to his new friend. However, Duncan found himself coming back to the painting over and over again in the next few days, up until he and his family left.

It wasn't until years later that he found himself at Huntington Park again. He was a young man then, and it was the summer holiday after his first year at Eton. He was fifteen, a little later than most boys who came to the boarding school, but it was necessary for him to ensure he could control his wolf before he went away. Oliver was a year ahead of him, and the Alpha had invited him to stay for a week before heading home to Scotland.

As the years passed by, he always thought that painting had been a figment of his seven-year-old mind's imagination. But, once again, he found himself roaming Huntington Park, until he found the storage room. Much to his surprise, the painting was still there and looked like it hadn't been moved at all in the last eight years. This time, he picked it up and placed it closer to the light, trying to scrutinize it and find out what it was that drew him to this painting.

"She's a pretty lady, huh?"

Duncan had felt himself turn red. "I, uh." He turned around to face the Alpha himself. "Your Grace. I'm sorry. I didn't mean to—"

"It's all right, my boy." The older Lycan smiled at him. "Ah, I remember her. My grandfather had her up in the parlor when I was young. I think my grandmother was a tad jealous and had her removed and put into storage." The duke stepped closer and peered at the portrait. "Those eyes are unusual, aren't they? And that grin—mischievous and mysterious at the same time. I've always wondered why the artist never finished painting her. Perhaps she died before he could. It wasn't unusual in those days."

"I suppose not." Still, the thought of her dying had sent his gut clenching. "Don't you want to display her anymore?"

"To be honest, I'd forgotten she existed," the old Alpha confessed. "But sometimes, it's nice to find old treasures like this." He looked at Duncan, his dark ebony eyes piercing into him. "If you were me, where would you put her?"

He thought for a moment. "I suppose I would put her in the library, so that everyone would see her."

The old Alpha's eyes sparkled, but he said nothing else.

Duncan couldn't remember how their conversation ended, exactly. But he did recall the next time he had seen the painting. It was two years later, and a large crate arrived at Castle Kilcraigh right after New Year's Day. His father had been puzzled because the sender was the estate of John Griffiths. The Alpha had passed away six months before, after all. They all gathered around, and when Callum broke the top open and took out an old framed canvas, he was even more perplexed.

"Why would the old man give me a painting?" he asked, scratching his head.

Kirsten peered at the document that arrived with the crate and began to read aloud. "'His Grace, the Duke of Huntington, bequeaths this painting to his dear friend, Duncan MacDougal, Viscount Warwick.'" His mother looked at him, her eyes wide. "Duncan? Did you know about this?"

Frankly, he was just as surprised as everyone else. He had only talked to the duke that one time. Did he know that Duncan had been fascinated by this lady for years?

In any case, as he told the old man, he displayed the portrait in the library, right over the fireplace where he could see her any time. And he did, whenever he went home during breaks between school terms or holidays when he visited while he was working in London. Now that he had been living in Castle Kilcraigh to help run the family distillery, he often took his afternoon coffee or tea under the watching, mysterious gaze of the lady.

Some time ago, an expert examined the painting, but they could only tell him that the style was probably Italian. There was no signature on the canvas, but the date and place where it was painted was scratched on the back—1820, Huntington Park, England. Though he'd gone back to England a few times to ask about the origin of the painting, no one there knew anything about it.

It seemed his overactive imagination was once again feeding his mind, because the lady was no longer just a painting. No, she was here, in his arms in the flesh. There was no way he was mistaken, not when he stared down at her beautiful mismatched blue and green eyes.

"It's you." He could hardly breathe. "It's really you."

Then it happened.

It was as if he was struck by lightning, then at the same time hit in the stomach by a cannonball while a sledgehammer slammed into his head. Heat, then cold, and then heat again spread all over his body. The strange thing was that the sensations didn't cause him any lasting pain.

Then his wolf let out a howl.

Mate, came a whisper from inside his head.

Well, fuck me.

But he was still staring down at her, his obsession come to life. And who, if he trusted his gut, was apparently his True Mate. He could feel her wolf, seemingly wary of him, but curious too.

Did she feel it too?

"Let go of me, asshole!"

Perhaps not.

"I—" But he didn't get a chance to say anything as she stomped down on his foot. He let out a yelp but tightened his hold on her, afraid that she would disappear if he let go. As she tried to shrug away, he got a whiff of her scent—shortbread cookies, ginger, and honey. Holy mother of God, it sent his wolf into a frenzy.

"Son? You all right? You're lookin' a wee bit dazed."

Duncan thought that voice was familiar. Who was it—oh, that was his father. They had arrived from a meeting in town when Mrs. Carter told them that their guests from America were here and having tea with Gerald in the library.

"Perhaps you should let the lass go?"

But he didn't want to. Despite the vicious, poisonous looks she was shooting him, he just couldn't. "No, I don't think so." The damn Devil himself could crawl out from hell before he let go.

Her eyes went wild. "Fucking asshole!"

Callum's brows were drawn together. "And why ever not?

"She's mine. My True Mate."

The room suddenly went silent and the revelation seemed to have shocked the young woman in his arms because she stopped struggling. "Excuse me?"

"You heard me." He grinned down at her. "You're my True Mate." Saying it out loud made his whole body feel light. Like he'd been holding a great secret his whole life, and now that it was out, it felt much better.

However, the she-wolf didn't seem to find that funny. Not at all, if the punch to the solar plexus he got was any indication. Doubling over in pain, he would have fallen to the floor had his father not held him up.

The woman looked around, confused, as if trying to find another exit. Fortunately for Duncan, the only door was located behind him, and there was no way he was going to let her get away. "You didn't feel it?"

Her adorable chin jutted out. "Feel what?"

"*Och*, why are you being daft, woman? You're my True Mate and that's that. Now," he grabbed her hand, his skin tingling as they made contact. "Tell me your name, darlin'."

"I am *not* your darling." She pulled her hand away. "And I am certainly not your mate."

"What are you saying?" Duncan ran his fingers through his hair. Did she not feel it too?

"Er, my boy." Callum stepped up beside him. "Remember what I told you? It doesn't work the same way for just any Lycan. Just our family."

Oh. *Right.*

Apparently, the wolves of Caelkirk recognized their mates immediately, and as far as they knew, it was a quirk that didn't exist in any other Lycan family. It had been the same for his parents, his uncles and aunts, as well as his grandfather and every member of the Caelkirk Alpha's family before that.

It wasn't something they talked about or anyone studied, but it was just a fact. He remembered his father telling him that his mother didn't believe him at first either, and that was after he had kept quiet, trying to ease her into the idea. In fact, she wasn't really convinced until it turned out she was pregnant—the only other way to tell if a pair were True Mates as their first coupling always resulted in a pregnancy.

Well, too bad, cat's out of the bloody bag now.

Callum must have had a good look at the girl, because his eyes went wide and his face turned confused. "But ... you ... how?"

His eyes drew back to the familiar portrait above the fireplace. The lady was still there, giving her mischievous smile. But somehow, with the real thing in front of him, the painting's beauty had faded. But, did she step out of the painting, like magic?

"Who are you?" he finally thought to ask.

Gerald, his father's younger brother and Beta, cleared his throat. "Callum, Duncan, these are our guests from America." He nodded to the other occupants in the room—a man with dark hair and an obviously pregnant redhead. "Mr. Reed Wakefield and his wife, Elise, daughter to the Alpha of San Francisco. And, uh, over there is Ms. Julianna Anderson, sister and envoy to the Alpha of New York. This is my Alpha and my brother, Callum MacDougal, Earl of Caelkirk and his son and heir, Duncan MacDougal, Viscount Warwick."

"Alpha," Reed came forward to greet Callum. "Thank you for allowing us into your territory...."

As they went through the formalities, Duncan found his gaze drawn to her again. *Julianna*. It fit her somehow. That face of hers, he knew well. But here, in the flesh, she seemed different. Her lips seemed plumper and rosier, and she was much taller than he would have imagined. She was slender and athletic, but the sweater dress she wore clung to her soft curves and his eyes traced the high, perky breasts, the dip into her small waist, and that ass—

The little chit hissed at him.

Looks like she wasn't going to come to him too easy. And

damned if the thought of a challenge actually made him want her even more. He wiggled his eyebrows at her, which only seemed to infuriate her.

"... you're very welcome here," his father said. "It's an honor to host you." He turned to Julianna. "And uh, I believe Lucas Anderson had said he was sending you so we could talk alliances."

She stiffened her shoulders. "Yes, Alpha. As you know, the matter with mages is a sensitive one. He thought it would be best if I were to come in person to explain."

Duncan opened his mouth to speak, but his father put a hand on his shoulder and pulled him back. "My son and I have business to attend to. Why don't you continue your tour and then we'll meet at dinner? Come along, sonny."

His wolf was loath to leave Julianna, but he knew she wasn't going anywhere, being that she was a guest and the envoy he and his father had been expecting. Besides, from the way his father practically dragged him out of the library, he knew there was no saying no to his old man.

"What was that all about now?" he exclaimed when they were far enough away for anyone to hear them.

"What was *that* all about?" Callum shot back. "Haven't you been listenin' to anything I've said over the years?" He gave his son a gentle smack on the back of his head. "I told you, when you meet your True Mate, you cannae just be shoutin' it at her like some *eejit* in love."

He rubbed his head. "*Och*, Da, that hurts."

"Aye right, it wasn't that hard. That lass was ready to skelp your face, which would have been worse." He led Duncan into his office, a couple of doors down from the library. "I know how it feels, sonny. You're suddenly struck with that feelin' and then your wolf wants you to claim her and make her yours. When I met your ma, I had to court her properly. Now, in the dark ages, it woulda been easy to just carry her off and make for the hills, but that's not how it works these days."

"I know that, Da." Duncan straightened his shoulders and tugged down on his jacket. "It's just that ... what was I supposed to do? Did you even look at her? See her face?"

"Aye, sonny." Callum sank down in his old leather chair. "It's strange isn't it? Her lookin' so similar to that lady of yours."

Julianna wasn't just similar. She was the lady's twin. If the painting wasn't over two hundred years old, he would have thought she'd posed for it. "It's eerie."

"But I suppose it makes sense. You've been obsessed—"

"I was not obsessed."

Callum raised a bushy white brow at him "I'm sure there's an explanation. But, I'm happy for you, sonny." His father stood up and walked over to his liquor cabinet and took out a bottle of their finest Scotch whiskey, Three Wolves 62 Single Malt, kept in a crystal decanter that was older than either of them. He poured a measure each into two glasses and handed one to Duncan. "I was gettin' worried you wouldn't meet your True Mate."

There was a warmth in his father's voice, but also a lot of implication. A True Mate meant pups, children to carry on the line. His wolf seemed to relish the idea of her having their pups, and Duncan couldn't deny the appeal, and it wouldn't be a chore. Julianna was even more gorgeous than the painting. Her olive skin looked petal-soft, and her slim body fit into his like they had been made for each other. She was perfect. And *his*.

He took a sip after they raised their glasses to toast, allowing the smooth liquor to make a warm path down his throat. "*Och*, are you gonna cry on me, you old fart?"

Callum laughed. "C'mon now. You've sowed your wild oats so much I thought you'd be startin' a sheep farm."

Duncan cringed inwardly. True, he had his fair share of women, and in his younger days, he had a wild streak that had gotten him in trouble. He couldn't help it if the female sex found him irresistible, and why would he, a single, healthy virile young man turn them down? Sure, he had broken a few hearts here and there, but he'd always been upfront with every woman he'd been with. No strings attached, no commitments. It wasn't his fault if they all thought they could be the one to change him.

And now, he'd found his mate, who seemed to check every box on his list, and she wanted nothing to do with him.

Karma, indeed, was a bitch.

"Don't you worry, son." Callum had probably guessed by the expression on his face what he'd been thinking. "She'll come around; they all do." He put down the glass. "But I have to say, I'll be enjoyin' the merry chase she'll be leadin' you on."

If the decanter of whiskey didn't cost thousands of dollars, he would have downed the entire thing. "What should I do, Da?"

"I know you're not used to goin' after lassies since they seem to naturally come to you, but now you're gonna have to woo her. And you might have to be sneaky about it."

"Sneaky?"

"*Och*, your Julianna looked like she was ready to run back to America if she had to."

That comment set his wolf on edge. The animal wanted nothing more than to just steal her away until she admitted she was their mate. Those Lycans back in the dark ages had it easy.

"Use your charm, sonny," he said. "Don't let those handsome looks of yours go to waste."

"There is a complication. She's the sister and envoy to the Alpha of New York." One of, if not *the* most powerful Lycan clans in the world, not to mention Grant Anderson, Julianna's father, was an influential member of the community.

"So, use that to your advantage. You're a smart lad, you know what to do."

Charming the panties off women, that he could do, but trying to win a mate? He'd never even had a serious relationship before. "Why doesn't she want to be my mate? Doesn't she feel the pull of being True Mates like I do?"

"It's not that she doesn't," he said. "She's your True Mate so she already feels that attraction to you. But she's not been raised like you and doesn't know how to listen to her wolf's desires, the way we and our ancestors have been doing for hundreds of years. It was hard enough to tell your ma about me bein' a Lycan, much less that she was the one that fate intended for me, and I was not going to have any other but her."

His mother, Kirsten, had been a human who was driving through Caelkirk when her car broke down. Callum happened to be passing by when he stopped to help her, and the rest, as they say, was history. But speaking of his mother ... "Do you think we could not mention this to Ma yet?"

Callum huffed. "Your uncle's a wee *clipe* and is probably spreading the gossip to the whole clan. I doubt we'd be able to keep this from anyone, let alone your ma or the rest of the family."

He groaned. "All right then, how do I go about wooing my mate?"

CHAPTER THREE

AFTER WHAT SEEMED LIKE THE LONGEST AND MOST uncomfortable tour she'd ever experienced in her whole life, Julianna was ready to lock herself up in her bedroom. No, scratch that. She wanted to take the next flight back to New York. Seeing as she hadn't yet unpacked, it would be easy enough to grab her suitcase, hop into the car, and drive away from this loony bin.

Because this was all crazy, right?

The initial shock of seeing Rossi's portrait hadn't even worn off before that boorish mountain of a man had his hands all over her and proclaimed them to be True Mates.

Insane.

"Uh, so, the Lupa will have dinner ready at seven," Gerald said as they re-entered the library after the two-hour tour of the house and grounds. "Kirsten will have a veritable feast prepared. We don't often get guests here. But it'll probably just be us family for now."

"Thank you, Gerald," Reed said. "The tour was excellent."

"It's an amazing place," Elise added. "Right, Julianna?"

Though the whole tour, Elise was doing her best to coax Julianna into the conversation, but she remained quiet, stewing and trying to avoid the curious looks Gerald had been giving her. "Yeah," she croaked. "It's a nice place."

"Glad you think so. I'll be off then." With a last nod, he left the library.

The moment the door closed, Elise dashed to Julianna and tugged on her sleeve. "Julianna? Are you okay? How are you feeling?"

She turned her head toward the other woman. "I'm ... fine."

"You just met your True Mate," Reed said. "You must be in shock. I sure as hell was when I recognized Elise."

Julianna shook her head. "It's not true, right? You ... your family ... I know Bridget and Eleanor said ..." Her thoughts were jumbled up. Was she even making sense?

"I'm afraid it is true." Reed placed a hand on her shoulder. "He's a descendant of my mother's family through Bridget and part of the Caelkirk clan, which means he did recognize you as his mate."

"But how?"

"I can't explain it, no one can." Reed paused. "All I know is that one moment everything was fine and then I looked into Elise's eyes, and the world was different." Elise blushed and he smiled fondly. "My wolf called her my mate."

"It's just ..." She paced for a few seconds, then stopped. Looking up, she came face to face with her likeness again. That damned painting. "What are we going to do about *this*?"

"Rossi's painting?" Reed asked. "What about it?"

"It's evidence! What if anyone found out about us? About *you*?"

He chuckled. "Julianna, how could anyone find out where I came from by looking at this painting? Besides, who would believe us anyway?" He raised a brow at her. "And don't try to change the subject."

Fuck. "I'm not. I'm just worried about keeping the fabric of space and time from ripping apart." No one could know about their time traveling experiences. It was too dangerous, and there was a risk that the mages would find out and try to use the dagger to travel back in time and change things.

"Look, maybe we're all just tired and jet lagged." Elise covered her mouth as she let out a yawn. "How about we get some rest and then get ready for dinner?"

Reed placed an arm around her protectively. "You must be exhausted, love. Let's go find our room so we can get refreshed." Turning to Julianna, his face turned soft. "Julianna, Duncan seems like a good chap. And you know, as your mate—"

"He's not my mate."

"I won't try to convince you." Reed let out an exasperated sound. "But I know that he would do anything to make you happy. And maybe ... maybe after all you've gone through, you deserve some happiness."

Julianna remained silent and watched them as they left the library. Reed's words had struck her. *Deep.* But happiness in a True Mate?

"Ha." Fat chance.

Sure, she'd seen her parents and some of their family members seemingly jubilant with their mates. But she wasn't her mother or Adrianna. No, she was far too independent, and she would never stand for it if a man tried to assert their dominance on her or acted like some possessive jerk.

She shivered, thinking of the way Duncan looked at her. Cocky jerk. His bright green eyes seemed to want to own every part of her. Well, she'd be damned before she let that happen.

The light outside was dying now, and the shadows seemed to subtly change the painting, staring down at her as if challenging her.

"Don't you think you know what's good for me," she said, pointing a finger at the painting. "I don't—ugh!" Throwing her hands up, she stalked away from the painting, and headed out of the library. Why the heck was she arguing with canvas and paint? Maybe the insanity of this place was getting to her.

"Damnit, Adrianna!" Julianna exclaimed as she tossed her open suitcase on its side, emptying the contents to the floor.

Fashion and clothes weren't her thing. Shopping was a chore and it only took her fifteen minutes to get ready in the morning. Usually, if she was going to the office, it was a dark colored skirt or pantsuit. If it was fieldwork, then she'd wear whatever she needed to blend in, like jeans or shorts. For formal occasions, she had a dozen black dresses from the same store. She could have sworn she packed at least two of them for this trip, but when she opened her suitcase, they were nowhere to be found. Instead, she found a sexy, low-cut red gown and a flirty blue-green cocktail dress. And heels. For fuck's sake, she didn't even own any shoes that were higher than an inch, and these were spiky black ones that made her look like some dominatrix.

There were only two people back in Jersey who could have messed with her clothes and she had a hard time thinking it was Darius rooting around in her underwear drawer. So, it had to be Adrianna. Her sister was always telling her she had the body of a supermodel, and she should flaunt it more often.

With a long sigh, she grabbed the blue-green dress, which was the lesser evil of the two. At least that one didn't have a slit that came up to her navel. After putting the dress on, she slipped her feet into the shoes. She found herself wobbling for the first couple of steps, but surprisingly, found her stride. *Huh, that wasn't bad at all.*

With one last glance at the mirror, she headed outside. Mrs. Carter had called over the intercom to tell her that there would be drinks in the parlor thirty minutes before the dinner. She checked her watch as she descended the stairs. *Damn.* She was five minutes late and so she rushed down the hallway on the right. The parlor was at the end of the gallery, Mrs. Carter had said, past the armory.

As she passed by a suit of armor guarding one door, she heard the sound of voices from the next room. Suddenly, she realized that she would not only have to face that *oaf,* but also the other people. Hopefully, no one had said anything about the mates thing or none of them believed it.

Placing her hand over her chest, she felt for the gold disc pressed against her skin. Lucas was counting on her, she reminded herself. *Forge the alliance.* Then get the fuck out of this loony bin.

As soon as she stepped inside the parlor, her eyes immediately were drawn to *him*. He was talking to his father and uncle, but it was like he sensed her presence the moment she walked into the room, as his head turned toward her. His sensuous mouth curled up into a grin and heat spread straight to her belly. Her wolf was rolling around, reveling in his attentions.

That stupid ass. Why did he have to be so goddamn sexy? He oozed sensuality, his green eyes darkening as he inspected her from head to toe. Earlier today, she didn't get a chance to just look at him as she was shocked and angry, but now, in the light of the chandelier, his hair looked more dark blond than the reddish blond she thought it was. That jacket he wore showed off his broad shoulders and tapered down to his trim waist and—holy hell, was he wearing a *kilt*?

"She's here!"

"Who?"

"Her! The American!"

"The one who looks like Duncan's painting?"

"His True Mate!"

Jesus. Motherloving. *Christ*. Surely it wasn't too late to back out of the room. And to leave the country.

A young woman rushed up to her and familiar green eyes looked at her expectantly. "Oh, she's so pretty! Like your painting." The owner of said eyes giggled, and for a second, Julianna thought Bridget was standing in front of her. However, she looked nothing like blonde and blue-eyed Bridget. No, this girl had wild red curls and green eyes, but the soft burr and laugh was the same. Her chest tightened, pressing into—

"I've been dying to meet you. I'm Roslyn MacDougal." She pulled Julianna into a hug. "I'm Duncan's sister."

"She's the baby."

Roslyn turned around. "I'm not a baby, Lachlan MacDougal! I'm sixteen—almost seventeen!"

"Really? What about all that baby fat all over your—*och!*" The man exclaimed as Roslyn reached over and pinched his arm. "Christ, woman! Those pincers are gonna get you in trouble." He turned to Julianna and smiled. "Well now, hello, lassie. Name's Lachlan MacDougal."

She took the enormous man's hand and shook it. Lachlan looked like a younger, brawnier version of Duncan. "Julianna Anderson." She tried to take her hand back, but Lachlan's grip was tight.

"So, you're Duncan's mate? Hmmm ... they said you look like the girl from the paintin' but ..." He moved closer until his face was inches away. "I'm not so sure. Is it your—"

"What in the bloody hell is going on here?"

Lachlan froze and turned his head but didn't let go of Julianna's hand. "*Och*, Duncan, I'm just trying to see if she's really the same girl—hey!" He staggered back and released her hand as Duncan pulled him away by the shoulder. "*Jaysus man*, you didn't have to pull that hard."

"Aren't you a big-shot MMA fighter? Surely it wasn't that painful?" Duncan's eyes blazed. "Don't think I don't know what you're doin'."

"'Cause you'd have done it yourself?" He ducked as Duncan swung at him. "*Oi*, stop! Stop!"

Duncan turned to Julianna. "Sorry about my youngest brother, he was born that way."

"Duncan!" said another voice.

"How about you introduce us to your mate?"

"I'm not his—"

Duncan rolled his eyes and stepped aside. "Julianna, these are my other brothers, Finlay and Fraser."

Julianna blinked. But she wasn't seeing double. The two men standing next to Duncan were definitely twins. Both had the same red hair as Roslyn, though kept short, and had blue eyes. "Julianna Anderson." She held out her hand, but the twins didn't make a move, looking at Duncan first who gave them a terse nod.

"Nice to meet you, lass," said Finlay—or was it Fraser?

"I hope you've been enjoying your stay so far?" Strangely enough, the other twin had a posher accent.

"Fraser's a professor of history in Cambridge," Duncan explained. "Finlay's our VP of production at the distillery."

Perhaps that explained the difference in the way they spoke, and Julianna realized that when she shook their hands, one of them definitely had rougher, work-hewn hands while the other's was smoother but callused at the thumb, like someone used to writing with a pen for hours.

"Oh, Duncan, is this her?" A sweet voice said. "Introduce me!"

Duncan's expression warmed as he pulled up the older woman behind him. "This is my mother, Kirsten MacDougal, Lupa and Countess of Caelkirk. Ma, this is Julianna Anderson."

"How do you do, Lady Caelkirk?" Julianna said. "Thank you for inviting us into your—"

The rest of her words were muffled as she found herself in another embrace. "We're not formal here. Please call me Kirsten. And you're my Duncan's mate!" Her smile was so bright Julianna wanted to wince. "I don't think you look like that painting at all."

"You don't?"

"Nay, you're much more beautiful. And I can't believe ... oh, Duncan!" Kirsten had tears in her eyes.

Callum walked up to them and put a hand around her shoulders. "I think I heard Mrs. Carter asking for you, my love. Somethin' about the roast." Before she could protest, her husband dragged her away.

"You did this on purpose," Julianna hissed at Duncan.

"Did what?" he asked innocently.

She huffed. "Tell everyone I was your True Mate."

"It's true."

"It's preposterous."

"Really? And how can you be sure I'm not telling the truth." He leaned down closer to her until his face was inches from hers. "D'you wanna give it a test?"

Heat crept up her neck. Oh, she knew exactly what he meant of course. The only real way to know for sure was if they had sex and she got pregnant right away. Her wolf seemed to like the idea of having a pup, but Julianna wasn't so keen. The sex part though ... that made her core clench.

"Ah, maybe you would like—"

"*Shut. Up.*" God, she wanted to smack that handsome face. It was a good thing Reed and Elise entered the parlor, as they were introduced to everyone in the room, and, to Julianna's relief, Kirsten was distracted because she was fawning over Elise, especially after finding out that she was pregnant with her True Mate's baby. Finlay handed Julianna and Reed a glass of whiskey and some juice for the expectant mom.

"Don't you worry, dinner will be ready soon," Kirsten said. "I bet you must be starving! I was all the time when I was pregnant with my children."

"I thought she was going to eat me out of house and home," Callum chuckled. "But, look at my boys. It's no wonder she was eatin' so much, eh?"

"Big strapping lads," Gerald commented. "The lot o' you. Me boys, too. We grow 'em big here."

"It's the genes," Reed commented, and he gave a sly smile to Elise.

Julianna, meanwhile, winced.

"Don't worry, dear, it might hurt a wee bit, but it's all worth it."

Much to Julianna's surprise, Kirsten was looking at her. "Excuse me?"

"I mean, when you have your own—"

"Isn't that food ready yet?" Callum interrupted. "We gotta get our guests fed or they'll be thinkin' we're poor hosts." He led his mate away, and everyone followed them toward a connecting door on the right side of the room.

God, I just want this night to end. Julianna downed the glass, allowing the smooth, smoky liquid to coat her throat. *Wow.* She was a vodka girl herself, but that was *good* whiskey.

"I know what you're thinkin'," a rich, velvety voice said in her ear. "And it's true what they say about kilts."

She stiffened, feeling a large hand at the small of her back. "What?"

"That we don't wear anything under it."

The man was insufferable. "I wasn't thinking that."

"But you are *now*."

The rough brogue made her shiver involuntarily, and—damn him—did make her think of what was underneath that kilt. As if reading her mind, he let out a throaty laugh and guided her toward the doorway, which led into a small, but elegant dining room. Though she tried to walk away from him and go to the opposite end, his hand snaked around her waist and pulled her toward a chair near the head of the table, then he sat down next to her.

Gritting her teeth, she sat down, not wanting to be rude. *This was it*, she thought. *We've only just met, and he was already acting like a possessive jerk.* She avoided his gaze, despite the fact that she could feel his eyes boring into her. She was just glad that Mrs. Carter and her staff had come in and begun serving the food.

"This really is the best whiskey I've had," Reed commented as he took a sip of the amber liquid from his glass. "You say you've owned this distillery for generations?"

"Aye," Callum replied. "Maybe two hundred years back. One of my ancestors actually came from another clan and married into Caelkirk, then brought the knowledge of distilling whiskey into the family."

"The Three Wolves was mostly a small batch distillery," Finlay added. "But in the last decade or so, demand has been increasing, especially in Asian markets, and we've had to expand a lot."

"Well, I hope I can purchase some," Reed said. "It's not too well known in America yet, but I bet with some marketing, you'll sell well there too."

"In that case, I'll give you case or two," Callum said. "Not many people can appreciate fine whiskey. You must have it in the blood. Maybe you do have a little Scottish in you?"

Reed nearly choked. "I, uh ..."

"That's what we're here for." Elise handed her husband a

glass of water. "My father spoke with you about Reed and how we were researching his roots."

"Oh, that's right." Kirsten clapped her hands together. "You poor dear. Abandoned as a child in a Yorkshire orphanage. And then those humans adopted you, right? How did you end up in America?"

"My father had a job offer in Canada." Reed put down the glass of water. "We moved when I was a teen. Then I was visiting the US when I met Elise."

"And you didn't know you were a Lycan until then?" Lachlan asked in a curious tone.

Reed shook his head. "It was a surprise."

Only a few people knew the truth of who Reed was and where he came from. Julianna had heard some of the story that had been crafted to make Reed's arrival into the modern and Lycan world more believable, but not the entire thing. She had to admit, it was genius saying that his wolf was latent. After all, her own Aunt Alynna had a similar story when she discovered later in life that she was a Lycan.

"I think he kind of looks like the old London Alpha." Duncan narrowed his eyes at Reed.

"Really?" Reed said smoothly, betraying nothing.

"Yeah. He's been gone a while, but I remember him having a similar chin. And he also had dark eyes."

"Maybe you were born on the wrong side of the blanket— ow!" Lachlan threw a dirty look at Roslyn who had hit him in the back of the head. "Fer feck's sake, Ros! We're eating."

"Don't be so rude, Lachlan." Roslyn stuck her tongue out at him. "And stop your whinin'. I'm surprised you haven't developed brain damage, seeing as we've all hit you so much."

"Why do you think he's a good fighter?" Fraser quipped.

Lachlan puffed up his chest. "You tell 'er."

"It's because he likes bein' beaten up, always has," Finlay finished, which earned him a dirty look from Lachlan.

"Oh, can't you all act civilized while we have guests?" Kirsten moaned and rubbed the bridge of her nose. "They're usually much better behaved when we have people over."

Finlay and Fraser chuckled, and despite her earlier mood, Julianna found herself smiling. This reminded her a lot of her own family, except that it was usually her and Isabelle fighting.

"Is that smile for me, darlin'?" Duncan was flashing her a teasing smile.

She returned it with a freezing stare. "No."

"You look so bonny when you're mad."

Did he ever give up?

"What—did I get you all tongue tied?" He leaned forward, reaching over her as if to make a grab for the dish of potatoes on her left, but made sure to brush against her. His scent permeated the small space between them and her wolf went wild.

Stop it, you horny bitch!

"I haven't even started. Should I show you how *I* keep my tongue tied up?"

Warmth rushed through her veins, and her wolf was practically sitting up and begging for him. *Fucking hell.* "Stop it," she whispered. "You need to get this straight into that thick skull of yours: I'm not your mate."

He gave her another infuriating smile. "Whatever you say, darlin'."

Julianna did her best to ignore him for the rest of the meal, instead, concentrating on her food. While he didn't try to converse with her, he did his best to make sure she never forgot he was beside her, whether that was brushing his thigh against her under the table or "accidentally" ensuring their hands touched when he asked her to pass something his way. Goddamn him, it was maddening, and her wolf *and* her body reacted to every little touch.

When everyone had finished dessert, Callum invited everyone for a nightcap in the library, but Elise had begged off because she was feeling tired. Reed didn't look like he wanted to end the night yet, seeing as he really looked like he was enjoying talking to the Alpha. Julianna couldn't blame him, as he probably was feeling nostalgic, but she also didn't let the opportunity pass her.

"I'll take her upstairs, Reed," she volunteered. "You go and have more whiskey. I'm feeling tired myself." She shot up so fast that her chair scraped loudly. "Don't worry, I'll make sure she gets into bed safe and sound." Walking around to their side, she helped Elise get up and practically dragged her out the dining room.

"You know, I'm not *that* tired," Elise said wryly.

"Shush, you're jet lagged and you're making a Lycan." She pointed her chin at Elise's bump. "It's exhausting. You're getting sleeeeepy."

Elise guffawed but also stifled a yawn. "You're just looking for an excuse to get out of there."

She neither admitted nor denied it. *It's his fault.* Stupid Duncan and his stupid sexy grins. Well, just because he seemed to think they were True Mates didn't mean she had to fall into that trap. No, she had her own mind, and genes or hormones weren't going to make her fall for that stupid ass.

CHAPTER FOUR

MORNING HAD COME TOO SOON, AND JULIANNA GROANED as she got up from the bed. Thank goodness the jet lag wasn't so bad, but the mattress was so comfortable, and she was having the most delicious dream that made her want to stay asleep longer.

Hmmm ... what was that dream about? Her sleep-fogged mind could only remember a few details, but she recalled being kissed all over by a warm, firm mouth and then looking down between her legs to see a pair of green eyes—

"Ugh!" The dream came rushing back vividly, and she tossed a pillow clear across the room. Goddamn him, she couldn't even get any peace in her sleep.

Fine, so she had dreamt that she got a peek under his kilt, but that didn't mean anything, except maybe she was horny, and it had been too long since she'd had any action down there aside from her vibrator. Pressing her thighs together, she felt the wetness and heat rush between her thighs. *Stupid dream.*

Deciding against relieving her tension with her fingers,

she got up and headed to the bathroom. Callum had requested to meet early because he had a lot of work, so they decided to have a breakfast meeting in his office, just the two of them. Whether it was because the Alpha had seen how uncomfortable she had been at his son's and family's attentions or if he really had a packed scheduled, she wasn't sure, but she was grateful to at least be able to get down to business without having to endure Duncan's attentions. Soon, though, she would be out of here, and she'd never have to see him again.

Shut up, she told her wolf when it let out an unhappy whine.

Feeling refreshed after her shower, she got dressed and left the room. There was a maid coming out of one of the bedrooms, so she stopped the young lady to ask for directions to Callum's office. Following her instructions, Julianna went down the same hallway as the dining room but stopped at the first door and knocked. A muffled "come in" came from inside.

"Alpha?" The smell of coffee and freshly-baked pastries were calling to her as soon as she entered. "I—what are you doing here?"

Duncan was sitting in the leather chair behind the large oak desk, grinning at her. "Good mornin', darlin'. Don't you look lovely today?"

His velvety voice caressed her skin. "Sorry," she mumbled. "I must have the wrong place. I'm looking for the Alpha's office."

Rising from his chair, he walked around the desk and headed straight for her, scratching at his beard as he eyed her.

"Oh, I think you're exactly where you're s'posed to be. This is the Alpha's office."

"Then what are you doing here?" she asked impatiently. "I have a meeting scheduled with your father."

"Like I said, you're exactly where you need to be." He straightened his shoulders. "Unfortunately, we had an incident at one of our facilities up north. Da had to leave early this morning."

"Seriously?"

"He's the president of Three Wolves Distillery, so he had to check on this personally."

Crossing her arms over her chest, she tapped her foot. "What time will he be back?"

"Time?" he asked. "He might not be back for a couple of days."

"A couple of days?" That was bullshit. "I have to leave for London the day after tomorrow."

"There was a serious accident. A couple of people were hurt."

"Oh." *Shit. Dammit!*

"That's why he asked me to meet with you." The corners of his mouth tilted up. "Which isn't really a hardship, you know."

"I'm supposed to meet with the Alpha," she pointed out.

"And I'm his heir, soon to be Alpha." Gently, he took her by the elbow. "He's asked me to conduct this meeting. He trusts my judgement. Besides, according to your brother, you're here to explain the situation to us and then he and my father will decide on the formal alliance." When she didn't budge, he trailed his fingers up her arm. "Of course, if you're willing to stay here longer and wait for him, I'm sure we could find ways to entertain oursel—"

"Fine." She shrugged his hand away, as the touch sent up unnerving jolts of electricity across her skin. "Let's get on with it." Being this close to him was too much. His scent was beckoning to her and her wolf, making her wonder what all that tanned skin would taste like, and *motherfucker*, her nipples tightened. It was that damn dream from last night.

As he moved back to the chair, Julianna couldn't help but notice how graceful he moved for a large man. She'd been around shifters her whole life, but Duncan was easily one of the tallest and broadest men she'd ever seen, built much like her brother-in-law Darius, but only an inch or two shorter than Cross. Today, he looked more relaxed in a black T-shirt which showed off the ink he had on his left arm. His powerful thighs were encased in jeans that seemed painted on. God, he was walking sex on a stick and her wolf was going crazy being in this enclosed space with him.

"Julianna, are you all right?" He cocked his head at her.

"Fine," she snapped. *Stop looking at his body!* When she focused on his face, it wasn't much better because her eyes immediately went to his mouth. He must have noticed because he smiled as he flicked his tongue out to lick his lips, and her goddamn clit practically *throbbed*. Fuck.

Focus on the task at hand, Julianna. He's just a man. Nothing special about him.

After giving herself a pat on the back for that pep talk, she squared her shoulders. Time to get down to business. Lucas was depending on her, after all. "I'm sure you and your clan know all about the mages."

He nodded. "Aye, but only from what I've read about that unfortunate incident thirty years ago."

That unfortunate incident, i.e. the Battle of Norway, had nearly killed most of her family, but she didn't want to digress. "The mages are back."

"We've heard that as well. At least this time, the high council isn't keeping it from us."

Back when her father was Alpha, it was the council's insistence to keep things quiet to prevent panic, not to mention that one of them had been working with their enemies, that had allowed the mages to gain power.

It was after the old council had been disbanded and a few of the bigger clans got together that it was decided the high council was to be run with more transparency. Perhaps they had grown lax because the mages hadn't shown themselves in three decades, but now since the mages reappeared, the high council was doing their best to spread the word and warn all the clans.

Julianna was just glad they were taking some action because it made her job easier. "And you've heard about the attacks in New York?"

"Aye, but not all the details." He leaned back into his chair. "Tell me what happened."

Julianna kept her tone neutral and business-like while she relayed the specifics of the initial attacks, up until the last one at Lucas's ascension, leaving out her time traveling adventure, of course. Duncan, too, had remained impassive, though she couldn't help but notice his hands curling into fists, particularly when she mentioned the incident in New Jersey when she, Adrianna, and their mother had been surrounded by dozens of Lycans who had been working for the mages.

"So, an alliance—"

"Is not even a question," Duncan said resolutely. "Consider it done."

A chill blasted across her skin at the power radiating from Duncan. She recognized it—the power of an Alpha wolf. While he technically didn't have the position yet, it was obvious he would be more than capable when that time came. Damn, if that power and competence didn't make her admire him. And maybe turned her on, just a little.

Okay, a *lot*.

Duncan got up and walked over to her side of the table. "I speak on behalf of my father, the Alpha. We will do whatever it takes to stop these mages."

"Thank you. I—" She frowned as she looked up at him. Her wolf bristled, sensing something wrong. His shoulders seemed tense, and the look on his face—he looked like he was barely holding on to his control. "Are you all right?"

His hands were stiff at his sides. "Julianna, I don't know how you can sit there calmly and tell me you nearly died twice and not expect me to react."

"That wasn't my intention." And then she sensed it—his wolf and the fury radiating from his animal. He winced, as if feeling it rip him up from the inside. To her surprise, he turned away from her and walked to the window.

She didn't know what possessed her, but she got up and followed, stopping just a step behind him. In the morning light, his dark blond hair looked like it was streaked with red, and she wondered what it would feel like between her fingers.

"I'm here. There's nothing to be angry about." She didn't know whether she was telling him or his wolf. "I can take care of myself you know. I've been doing it for as long as I can remember. I work for the Lycan Security Force of my clan." She was proud of what she had accomplished and all the people she helped.

"Does your job always put you in danger?" He didn't look at her, but kept his face turned toward the outside.

"Sometimes." She waited for it. The way other Lycans always reacted when she told them she worked in a tradition-ally male-dominated field. It was either disbelief, or they thought the only reason she got in was because she was the Alpha's daughter.

"I don't like it, but I have to respect that you wouldn't have that job if you weren't capable."

Disbelief stunned her. She had thought he was going to go ballistic and demand that she stop putting herself in danger immediately like some possessive he-man jerk. "Thank you."

It unnerved her though that he still wouldn't look at her. Her wolf, too, was crying out, wanting to make sure he was fine. "Is there anything I can do to ..." What exactly? Help him?

"Well, now that you mentioned it." He turned around quickly, nearly bumping into her. "How about going on a picnic with me?"

"Picnic?" That came totally out of left field.

"Yes. Later today, for lunch."

"But—"

"I saw Elise and Reed this morning and mentioned it to them and that I wanted to show you all the grounds. They've already said yes." Without waiting for her to say anything, he walked toward the door. "I have some work to do before then. I'm glad we had this talk. We can speak more about the alliance later."

She stared at him, her jaw dropping. Hold on. Did he just—

He did, the *bastard*.

Just who did he think he was? Who the hell was he?

"Ugh!"

Reaching for a morning roll, she stuffed half of it in her mouth, then swallowed it down with a gulp of coffee. At least she wasn't going to be alone with him. He really was confusing. Last night he had been charming, this morning he oozed with raw sexuality, and then he acted like he cared what happened to her and upset that she had almost died.

Sexist jerks and childish men, she could handle. But if he kept switching up on her like Jekyll and Hyde, she didn't know how she would handle him.

———

It was cool in the Highlands, but Julianna didn't need to bundle up as her Lycan body naturally adjusted to the weather. Still, it was nice, after the long hot summer, to be able to put on her flannel shirts, leggings, and boots for this picnic Duncan had somehow manipulated her into going to. She wasn't sure where to meet, so she ended up downstairs in the foyer just before noon. Elise and Reed were already there waiting for her.

"Did you have a good morning?" Elise asked.

"Yeah." She updated them on what happened during the meeting with Duncan.

"Looks like your first foray as an envoy went well," Reed commented. "Not that we had any doubts, of course."

"Thanks." Her troubles with the stubborn Lycan aside, the meeting really wasn't that bad. In her years as part of the special investigations division, she'd met all kinds of people and was comfortable speaking to almost anyone. While she preferred fieldwork, if this is what it took to unite the rest of the Lycan world and defeat the mages, then it was something she was willing to do.

"Oh, good, you're all on time." Duncan strolled up to them looking so relaxed in the same outfit he wore this morning.

"Thank you for inviting us," Elise said. "Although I won't be able to walk too far or too fast."

"No worries, I've taken care of our transport." He looked at Julianna. "Ready?"

She swallowed, trying not to let that sensual, lazy grin affect her. "As I'll ever be."

They followed him outside where, much to her surprise, there was a golf cart waiting, the back loaded with two large baskets.

"It's much more comfortable than walking, and this way we can cover more ground." Duncan walked over to the driver's side as Elise and Reed climbed into the back. Seeing as there was only room for two in the rear seat, she climbed up front next to Duncan. He flashed her another grin that made her heartbeat pick up. Turning her body away from him, she looked out to her side, admiring the beauty of the Highlands, the rolling hills, and the purple-gray heather dotting the landscape. Though she did her best to ignore him, she couldn't help but feel Duncan's eyes on her every once in a while. Fifteen minutes later, the golf cart stopped right by a line of trees.

"Here we are." He turned off the engine, then walked to the back of the golf cart to grab the wicker baskets. "This way."

He led them through a small forest of trees, and they came out on the other side to a beautiful clearing. Being early fall, everything was still green though there were some dots of orange and red in the distance. Above them, the sky was a perfect blue, with big fat clouds floating by.

"Amazing," Elise said. "It's so beautiful out here."

Beside her, Reed nodded in agreement. "Breathtaking."

Julianna drank in the gorgeous view and allowed herself to marvel in what was around her. Having grown up in the city, she wasn't used to this kind of landscape. Even New Jersey, her mother's home base, didn't have this wild beauty.

"It certainly is breathtaking." She stiffened when she felt Duncan's presence behind her, but that didn't stop the thrill of sexual energy running through her when his warm breath caressed her cheek. "And the view's good too," he added.

Ugh, this man! Whirling around, she crossed her arms over her chest. "I was promised lunch."

"Of course, darlin'." His voice was like thick honey. "I always keep my promises." Hauling the baskets to a shady area, he began to unpack them, taking out plates, napkins, and containers of food.

"I'll go help him. Why don't you two relax?" Reed walked over to Duncan, leaving Elise and Julianna alone.

"Are you really not going to give him a chance?" Elise asked. "You know he set this whole thing up for you."

"Set this up for me?" Her nose wrinkled. "He said you guys had accepted his invitation this morning before our meeting."

"Uh, no. He came to us about an hour ago and asked us to come."

She crossed her arms under her chest. "That's not what he said."

"Ah, I see." Elise's mouth curled up into a smile. "You really don't think you're True Mates? Your wolf doesn't feel anything at all? Doesn't want him on any level? Doesn't get distracted by his scent?"

She opened her mouth, then shut it quickly. "What does that have anything to do with it?"

"He's certainly handsome. And so big and sexy and—" The involuntary growl coming from Julianna stopped her. "My, my, your wolf didn't like it when I called Duncan handsome and sexy—"

"Oh, not you too!" Julianna put her hands up in frustration.

"I really don't understand why you keep denying it." Elise's electric blue eyes sparkled. "He's perfect for you."

"It would never work out." She puffed out a breath. Elise wouldn't understand. Besides, how was this going to end up? Was she supposed to move here and start popping out babies? Did Duncan expect her to give up her job, her family? And what about the mages? No, every hand they could spare was needed in this fight. The moment the mages came back and threatened her family, she knew she was going to see this to the end.

"I think it's time to eat." Elise's chin pointed toward the two men, who were waving them over. "I'm starving. Let's go."

They walked over to the picnic area and Elise, of course, sat down next to Reed at the edge of the large tartan blanket, which meant the only spare spot was beside Duncan on the other end. His smile was as wide as the Brooklyn Bridge when she sat down next to him, though she positioned herself as far away from him as possible.

As they ate the delicious prepared lunch of sandwiches and pastries, Julianna prepared herself to be assaulted by Duncan's charm and cheesy lines, but to her surprise, he turned to Reed and began to ask him questions, drawing him into a conversation about possibly bringing Three Wolves Whiskey into the US market. In fact, he seemed to be ignoring her.

"... I could speak to my father-in-law." Reed put his plate down. "His family's company supplies a lot of restaurants in California. I'm sure he could get you some contacts."

"That would be great." Duncan poured some whiskey from a flask and handed it to Reed. "We're getting noticed in Asia, but the US market would be big for us."

"Do you travel to Asia a lot?" Reed asked. "I've always wanted to see the Orien—I mean, that continent." Elise looked like she was trying not to laugh at her husband's use of the very non-PC term, and Julianna bit her lip to do the same. It really was weird seeing Reed in modern clothes and inter-acting with other people in their time. She wondered if he had made any other faux pas when he first came here.

"As Executive Vice President, I have to," Duncan said. "I go to Shanghai, Tokyo, Seoul and a few places here and there, but I don't really get to see the cities I go to. It's mostly boring business meetings and dinners."

"Reed," Elise patted her husband's arm to get his attention.

"Love?" Reed immediately placed his hand on her stomach. "Are you all right? Is it the pup?"

"No ..." She whispered in his ear and his face changed.

"Oh. Right." He turned to Duncan. "I don't suppose you have any ... er, facilities near the area?"

"'Fraid not. Sorry, I didn't think about that ..." He scratched his head. "Er, why don't we go back? We can have some fresh, hot tea and finish dessert inside."

"Oh no! It's such a lovely day," Elise said. "How about we just quickly drive to the castle and come back again? No need to interrupt our lunch."

"There's a shorter way back," Duncan said. "Shouldn't take more than five minutes if we take that path."

Julianna got up and brushed the crumbs off her lap. "I'm gonna take a walk." It was a beautiful day, and she wasn't ready to go inside. "I ate way too much. I'll meet you all back here in half an hour." With a wave of her hand, she trudged off in the direction of the sloping hill on the east side of the clearing.

Glad for the time alone, Julianna took a deep breath, enjoying the fresh air and the scenery. When she got to the top of the hill, she saw a small body of water not too far away and decided to investigate. A few minutes later, she reached it and realized it was a pond. While it seemed clean, the dark blue water indicated it was much deeper than it first looked.

"Ah, you've found my favorite spot in all of Caelkirk."

"*Jesus Christ on a bicycle!*" Her heart nearly burst out of her chest in surprise. "What the hell are you doing here? Are you following me?"

Duncan gave her another one of his mega-watt grins. "I do live here, you know."

She pointed back to the direction of the picnic area. "I thought you were driving Elise back to the castle?"

"I was, but Reed was keen to drive the golf cart. I told him it was much easier than drivin' a car, and after I showed him the basics, he felt confident enough to go back without me."

That traitor. And she bet Elise didn't really have to go to the bathroom. "Well, I have to go too, so maybe we can—"

"What's the matter? Are you afraid to be alone with me, Julianna?"

God, she wanted to wipe that smirk off his face!

He laughed and reached over to tuck a stray piece of hair behind her ear. "I know I'm irresistible, but I can trust my virtue is safe in your hands."

Callused fingertips brushed her skin, making heat coil in her middle. "Look here, Duncan. I'm not here to play games."

"And who said I was playin' games?" His tone lowered. "I'm serious, Julianna. Serious about you."

"Stop! This is crazy."

"Crazy?" He took a step closer to her. "What do I have to do to prove to you how serious I am about you?"

"Prove to me ..." He really was mad! "There's nothing. Nothing you can do."

"*Och*, darlin' you wound my heart." He placed his hands over his chest. "If you don't care about me, then this life isn't worth living."

"Now you're mocking me." The way he changed from

charming to serious to mocking made it hard to figure out what his deal really was.

"I'm not." Looking around, he cocked his head toward the pond. "In fact, I'm so serious about you, I'll jump in this pond."

"Jump in the pond?" she said incredulously. "Do you even know how to swim?"

"We'll find out, won't we?"

"Find—" A loud splash cut her off. *Idiot!* He really did jump!

She tapped her foot as she waited for the dumbass to surface. Small bubbles formed over the spot where he'd jumped, but the water remained unbroken. A few more seconds passed before panic began to seep in. "Duncan?" Oh God, what the hell was happening with him? Did that idiot not know how to swim? "Duncan!"

Before she could change her mind, her body propelled forward. The cold, icy water hit her like a thousand little needles, but she ignored it. Her wolf clamored for her to find him and make sure he was okay. Kicking her feet, she dove down further—how deep was this fucking pond?—and as her Lycan eyes adjusted to the darkness, she saw a figure inches away. Reaching out, her hand grasped a solid, muscled arm. She held on tight and kicked for the surface as hard as she could.

After a few strokes, she broke the surface, taking in a large gulp of air, then swam toward the edge. With her Lycan strength, it was easy to drag Duncan up to the muddy shore, but his bulky, wet body made it an awkward task.

She knelt next to him and pressed her hand on his chest. His eyes were closed and his skin was cold. "Fuckity, fuck,

fuck!" Leaning down, she opened his mouth to check if he was breathing. "Duncan? Duncan, please don't die!"

His eyes remained shut, but his lips trembled. "*Och*, you do care about me, Julianna."

"What—" Her protest came too late as a hand snaked around her nape and pulled her down, her mouth pressing against his.

She struggled, but his grip was too strong. And his mouth was too warm. And his lips too insistent as they moved under hers. Yeah, that was totally the reason she didn't stop him when he kept on kissing her or when his hand moved lower to her back. Before she knew it, Duncan had rolled her over so she was under him.

Despite the chill of the wet clothes, her entire body seemed to be on fire. His damned lips kissed her expertly, coaxing her mouth to open and let his tongue dip in past her teeth. She should have bitten it off, but his masculine scent was sending off signals in her brain like an overactive switchboard, firing off sensations all over her body she'd never felt before. And his taste ... smoky and earthy like the fine whiskey he'd been drinking earlier, but mixed with something that she knew was unique to him.

No, I don't want this.

Yes, you do, her slutty body replied.

A hand pulled her wet flannel shirt up, and fingers skimmed over her ribcage, slipping under her bra to cup her breast. He pressed his hips down, and she felt his hardness pressing up against her core, making her squirm. That only encouraged him, nestling him further until the ridge of his cock lined up perfectly against her, and zings of pleasure fired off across her body. Arching into him, she moved her hips, seeking that pleasure her body craved.

A discreet cough made them both freeze.

"Don't mind me now," said the familiar, masculine voice. "I'm just here for the free show."

Duncan snarled against her mouth. "Fuckin' Lachlan." He pulled her up so fast that she nearly tumbled back when her head spun. His arm snaked around her and pulled her against his body. "What the hell are you doin' here?"

Lachlan was sitting in the driver's seat of the golf cart, an amused grin on his face. "Sorry to, uh, disturb your little outing." He winked at Julianna, which only made Duncan tuck her tighter against his body. "Mrs. Carter sent me to find you. We're needin' you back at the house."

His entire body tensed. "Is there something wrong? Anyone in trouble?"

"You can say that." Lachlan chuckled. "Royally big trouble."

Duncan's brows knitted. "Royally big—fucker!" His hand scrubbed down his face. "Now?"

Julianna's head ping-ponged back and forth between the brothers. What was going on?

Lachlan nodded. "From that dumbstruck look on your face, I can guess this was an unplanned visit."

A string of curses flew out of his mouth.

"C'mon now," Lachlan laughed. "Can't keep our guest waiting then."

CHAPTER FIVE

"I'm going to kill him," Duncan muttered under his breath. "I'm really going to kill him."

"Are you sure that's a good idea?" Lachlan asked as he turned into the driveway leading to the front of the castle. "I thought he's your best friend?"

"I don't give a fuck."

Talk about having the *worst* timing in the world. *God, I should wring his neck!* He glanced back to look at Julianna, who was sitting in the back seat, the picnic blanket wrapped around her. From the way her body and head were turned away from him, it was obvious she was still angry. Oh, and there was that murderous look she gave him earlier. But at least their relationship was progressing.

Sure, it was dastardly of him to trick her like that, but he had to prove to her he was serious. It was disconcerting that it took her a minute to jump in after him, but it was worth the wait. Especially now that he'd had a taste of her. And he wanted more, and he was going to get more. He would have her, all of her, soon, or he would very well go insane. At least he'd proved one thing: though she may deny it, Julianna definitely wanted him as much as he wanted her. Too bad they were interrupted by his unexpected guest.

The golf cart stopped in front of the castle, and Julianna dashed out. But Duncan was faster, and he reached her just before she slammed the door in his face.

Pushing through, he grabbed her wrist just as they both stepped into the foyer. "D'you think you could keep me out of my own bloody home, woman?"

"You lied to me," she hissed.

"Lied to you?" He tugged her closer. "When have I ever lied to you, darlin'?"

"You said you couldn't swim!" Her tone was full of indignation. "Which is why I jumped in after you."

"I never said I couldn't swim," he reasoned. "I said you would find out if I did."

"I should have let you drown." She struggled harder now as she attempted to get out of his grasp. "Let me go!"

"It seems the gods have answered my prayers," said a heavily-accented voice. "Beautiful women are now trying to get away from you, instead of throwing themselves at your feet."

Duncan didn't turn his head toward the speaker, already knowing who it was. Instead, he focused on Julianna who stopped struggling. Her dark brows knitted together in confusion.

He let her wrist go, then turned his head toward the new arrival. "What the fuck are you doin' here?"

"Tsk, tsk, is that any way to talk to royalty?"

"Oh, sorry," Duncan mocked. "Forgive my manners.

What the fuck are you doin' here, *Your Highness.* Is that better?"

Prince Karim Idris Salamuddin laughed. "Hello, old friend, it is good to see you."

Duncan reached his hand out, and the two men clasped each other by the arm. "How are you, my friend?" Though the visit was unexpected, Duncan, of course, didn't resent his best friend coming even though his time with Julianna had been interrupted.

"As well as I could be." His eyes focused somewhere behind Duncan. "Who is your guest?"

Duncan almost forgot about Julianna, and he was surprised she was still there. However, seeing the way Karim's eyes raked over her with interest, he almost wished she did run away.

Clearing his throat, he pulled her forward, snaking an arm around her shoulder. "Julianna, allow me to introduce His Royal Highness, and royal pain in my ass, The Crown Prince Karim Idris Salamuddin, Heir to the Throne of Zhobghadi. Your Highness," he tried not to laugh when he used the formal salutation. "This is Ms. Julianna Anderson of New York."

Karim put on his most dazzling smile. "Lovely to meet you, Ms. Anderson." He took the hand she offered and kissed it. As he let go, he looked up at her, his head cocking to the side. "Have we met before?"

Julianna stiffened. "I don't think so."

Duncan's wolf nearly leapt out of him, but he reined it in. Despite his earlier threat of murder, he really couldn't do it to his oldest friend. Instead, he lowered his arm around her waist, resting his palm on her hip.

A dark brow lifted at the possessive gesture. "So, you've finally decided to bring one of your girlfriends home to meet your family?"

"I'm not his girlfriend." Julianna shoved him away. "If you'll excuse me, I'm going to catch a cold if I don't get changed out of these wet clothes." She pivoted and marched up the staircase.

When she disappeared from view, Karim said, "Anything you care to tell me?"

"It's a long story. One best told over some whiskey."

The prince laughed. "Now you are talking."

As the two men walked together, Duncan decided to get a few things out of the way before they relaxed. "I'm sorry about your father."

Karim's face didn't falter at all, but Duncan could see the prince's cerulean blue eyes turn dark. "Thank you. I have received your messages and voicemails but—"

"You're busy, I understand." And he did, really. It couldn't have been easy to lose your only parent so suddenly, without warning. From what Karim had told him before, King Nassir was strong and healthy, showing no signs of illness. To hear that he had died of a sudden heart attack was shocking to say the least. "I'm always here for you, my friend."

"I know. And I am sorry to come unannounced."

"You know you're always welcome here. It's been too long since you last visited Castle Kilcraigh."

Karim rubbed his thick dark beard with his thumb and forefinger. "Was it ... five years ago?"

"Six, at least. I was still working in London at the time. You came for Christmas."

"Ah, much too long then."

They stopped just outside the library, and with Karim being so comfortable at Castle Kilcraigh, he went inside first. When his eyes landed on the painting over the mantle, Duncan realized he should have warned him at least.

The normally unflappable prince looked gobsmacked. Slack-jawed, he turned to Duncan, then to the painting, then back to Duncan. "You have some explaining to do, my friend."

Duncan gestured to the couch, then walked over to the liquor cabinet to grab a decanter and two glasses. Pouring a measure for each of them, he stalked back to the sitting area and handed a glass to Karim. How was he going to explain it to him? Karim was human after all and knew nothing about Lycans and True Mates. He took a big gulp of whiskey before speaking. "She's a guest of my family, from another cla—another company. Here on business."

Karim wrapped his hand around the glass and stared into the amber liquid. "And her resemblance to your lady? How did this come to be?"

"Damned if I know." And damned if he cared. Duncan wasn't a religious man, but if this wasn't a fucking sign they were meant to be together, then he didn't know what this all meant. "The experts I hired to check the painting couldn't really tell me anything except that the painter was most likely Italian."

"An ancestor perhaps? I've seen some portraits of old and can trace the similarities to the descendants. But still ... the resemblance is stunning." Karim took a sip from his glass.

"That's the weird part." Duncan scratched his head. "The painting was done in England."

"Quite a conundrum." Karim shrugged. "But you know they say that sometimes the simplest explanation is the truth. It is a coincidence."

Duncan nodded in agreement, but the feeling that there was another explanation just kept niggling at him.

The prince's brows drew together. "So, your real flesh and blood lady ... she doesn't want you?"

Duncan laughed at his friend's surprise. Karim, after all, had been his frequent companion when they'd trawled the bars in their younger days. "Oh, she wants me." That kiss— and more—this afternoon proved it.

Karim looked at him over the rim of the glass as he took another sip. "She just doesn't want anything else to do with you."

"She's a ... challenge."

"A first for you."

"She'll come 'round." *She had to.* Uncomfortable with where this was going, he decided to change the subject. "To what do I owe this surprise visit, by the way?"

Karim put the glass down on the table. "I do apologize for showing up unannounced. I just ... I needed to get away. The paparazzi are getting on my nerves. The *Almoravid* actually found one of them hiding in the trunk of my limo," he said, referring to the elite members of the Zhobghadi Military who served as personal protectors to the royal family. "I can't go anywhere without the press following me."

"Finally catchin' up with you, you mean?" While in their younger days, Duncan had been far worse when it came to partying and women, he did manage to straighten himself out since he'd moved back to Scotland. Karim, on the other hand, not only continued his jet-setting playboy ways, but because of his status, developed a very public reputation. The gossip rags were filled with ink devoted to his supposed escapades with various supermodels, actresses, and socialites all over the world. Most of the things they printed were wild speculations and outright lies, but Duncan knew his friend enough to know there was some truth to those stories.

"I suppose everything catches up eventually." His eyes turned dark. "We took a roundabout way here and shook them off our tail. They'll never guess this is where I came. I just need some peace. I will be leaving in the morning, however. I must return to Zhobghadi."

"So, are you finally taking the crown?" Though he hadn't spoken to his friend in almost a year, he had read on the news —real political news, not gossip rags—that the throne of Zhobghadi still sat empty, and a coronation had not been announced. Whether that was deliberate, Duncan didn't know, but he knew his friend was not expecting to become king so soon and had enjoyed his life of leisure.

Karim grunted. "It is complicated. But once I return this time ... things will be different. I may not have the opportunity to visit you again."

Duncan understood. Once Karim was king, he would have many responsibilities as the head of state. Random jaunts to Scotland wouldn't be possible. "I appreciate you wanting to spend your last moments of freedom with me. Your timing is shite," he chuckled. "But I'm glad you're here."

Karim gave him a warm smile. "So, tell me all about your Julianna."

His Julianna. He liked that. She wasn't yet his, but she would be. "Where do I begin? You know, she stomped on my foot and punched me in the stomach the first time we met...."

———

Duncan spent most of the afternoon catching up with Karim, not an unpleasant time, though his mind kept wandering off to thoughts of Julianna, where she was and what she was doing. He knew she probably needed some time to cool off, though even now, all he wanted to do was hunt her down and taste those plush lips of hers again. The feel of her body underneath his had been so right, and he knew if he didn't have her soon, he was going to go crazy.

Unfortunately, since he had wiled the afternoon away, his work began to pile up. His parents agreed to head up north so he would have an excuse to be alone with Julianna, but that meant he was stuck doing his father's work too. As soon as he was done, though, his first thought was to seek out Julianna. But, unsure if the she-wolf was still mad at him—and odds were she probably was—he switched tactics and went to Reed and Elise instead. He told them that since his parents were gone and took Roslyn with them and that Fraser had gone back to England, the remaining people at the castle could go into town for dinner, at a local pub named The Black Swan. They thought that was a good idea and said they would relay the message to Julianna.

To his surprise, Julianna showed up downstairs at the appointed time and even volunteered to drive their rental so they wouldn't all have to squeeze into his Land Rover. When they got to the pub, however, she sat as far away from him as possible and gave him cool, indifferent looks when he tried to include her in the conversation. It annoyed him no end, but he had faith that they wouldn't be True Mates if she didn't feel anything for him at all. Sure, they had only met yesterday, but her reluctance was maddening. It was like she didn't even want to try. His wolf was urging him to make her theirs, but it was difficult to reason with the animal that it wasn't as simple as making off into the hills with her.

After they finished dinner, Lachlan declared he wanted a couple of pints at the bar. Karim joined him, as did Finlay.

"How about it?" he asked the Americans as the rest of their party had already gone to the bar.

"Go ahead, Reed," Elise encouraged her husband. "I'll be fine. You know I can't stand alcohol in my condition."

"I'll stay with her." Julianna raised her glass of wine. "I'm not done yet."

"All right." Reed stood up. "It has been a while since I've gone to a real public house—I mean, *pub*."

Duncan shook his head mentally. Reed Wakefield was a strange one. He was well-mannered, in fact, rather too well-mannered sometimes. And sometimes he'd say strange things and spoke like he was in a Shakespearean play. He liked the man, though.

However, there was something about Reed ... Duncan just couldn't figure it out. Like, underneath that cool surface was something he was trying to hide or keep inside. But if he was anything like his English relatives, he wasn't the type to let it out. Hopefully, the man would find some outlet for his feelings before he exploded.

When they approached the bar, Lachlan handed them two pints. "Here you go."

"Thank you." Reed seemed taken aback by the sheer size of the mug. "I must say, it's been a while since I've had a real pint of ale—er, lager."

Finlay laughed. "All that time in North America's softened you up."

"You are not English?" Karim asked. "But you sound and act so English."

"Reed was born in England, but emigrated to Canada when he was a teen," Duncan explained. He had introduced Elise and Reed to him before they came here, but failed to tell his friend of their background. "He's researching his ancestors because he was adopted."

"Ah, and how goes this research?"

"Very well, Your Highness." Reed took a big gulp from his pint. "So, tell me," he gestured with his glass toward Karim and Duncan. "How did a foreign prince and a Scotsman become best friends?"

"We had common enemies." Karim grinned.

"At school," Duncan clarified. "We were both fifteen, came in weeks apart at Eton, me at the beginning of the year and him sometime in the middle."

"We were the foreigners," Karim said. "All those stuffy English boys hated us. That's why we got along."

"And he was the only bastard as large as me at that age," Duncan added.

"I'm still taller," Karim added smugly.

"And he never lets me forget it." *Ah, those were the days.* "Those dandy boys picked on us, so we banded together against the *fookin' English*." He turned to Reed. "No offense."

The other man chuckled. "None taken. But it certainly is an interesting friendship."

"Duncan is like a brother to me," Karim confessed and raised his glass toward Duncan.

He was taken aback, but clinked his pint against Karim's and took a drink. "Thank you."

Those words meant a lot, and he knew Karim wouldn't ever say them lightly. His friend was very closed off, and while he may consider Duncan a brother, he knew there were certain things the prince would never confide in him. While many people thought Karim had won the genetic lottery by being born a prince, it sounded more of a burden than a gift, especially when he talked of growing up lonely in the palace with no siblings close to his age or friends. Then there was that dreadful business about the mysterious death of his mother, a fact that many gossip rags loved to muck up every now and then.

"*Och*, are we gonna start cryin' like old biddies now?" Lachlan guffawed. "Shall I go get me mum's knitting needles, and we can start a fucking quilting circle?"

The men laughed, and as if to prove Lachlan wrong, ordered another round, which they all decided to down in one gulp, racing to see who could finish first. They did this a few more times. As Lycans, they burned through the alcohol quickly, but after the fourth round, Duncan was definitely feeling a little buzzed.

"You have the constitution of a Scotsman," Finlay remarked as he watched Karim down one more pint. Indeed, Karim was the only human he knew who could drink him and his brothers under the table.

"This swill you call beer?" Karim slammed the glass down on the bar. "It is nothing. I should bring you some of our special drinks from Zhobghadi." He looked around, then nodded in the direction of the men's room. "Excuse me, I'll be right back."

"You know," Lachlan began when Karim was far enough away, "we need to give our friend some of that special brew." He wiggled his eyebrows.

"Special brew?" Reed asked.

Duncan grinned. "Yeah. It's something we've been working on for a better part of the year. A whiskey that can get even Lycans drunk."

"Truly?" Reed seemed intrigued. "What's in it?"

"Well, we've got a special—What's wrong Lachlan?"

His brother's smile had transformed into a scowl. "That."

Turning around, he followed the direction of Lachlan's glare. Elise and Julianna were still sitting at their table, but they were not alone. Two men were sitting down with them, and one of them was next to Julianna, leaning in close.

"What the fuck is that scabby bassa doing?" Lachlan slammed his glass on the bar top. "You gonna let that bawbag put his hands all over your mate?"

Duncan was already marching toward the girls, and Reed was right behind him. He could feel the other man's wolf practically leaping out. The second man was trying to talk to Elise, despite her body language screaming her discomfort and the fact that she was obviously pregnant. He couldn't blame Reed because his own animal was ready to rip some heads off.

"... can't believe any man would let pretty lasses like you all alone."

Julianna's eyes narrowed at him. "I don't need—"

"They're *not* alone." His voice was even, despite the turmoil he felt inside.

The man pretended like he didn't hear Duncan. "How about we go to my place and—"

His fingers itched, but he kept his hands at his sides. "Listen here—"

"Stop." Julianna rolled her eyes and held up a hand. "I'm not going anywhere with you."

"You're bloody right, you aren't," Duncan said. "She's m—"

"And you listen here, Duncan," Julianna interrupted. "I can take care of myself. You don't have to act like some white knight who—" A loud crash cut her off and made her start.

"I said get the bloody hell away from my WIFE!" It seemed Reed wasn't taking no for an answer either as he had grabbed the man who was sitting next to Elise and threw him across the room, sending him crashing against the wall.

"Fookin' English bastard!" someone screamed. "Git him!" Chairs scraped and tables were pushed over as a room full of drunk Scotsmen zeroed in on Reed.

Duncan had been so distracted that he didn't see the man next to him pull his fist back, aiming for his head. He braced himself for the hit, but it never came.

Julianna moved so fast; she was just a blur. One moment she was sitting down, and the next, she had the man's face down on the table, his hands pinned behind him.

"I said, I'm not going anywhere with you, asshole," she growled.

Bloody hell, he was scared and turned on at the same time.

"*Och*, stupid cunt!" He screamed when Julianna twisted his hand. "Bitch!"

Duncan lost it and planted his fist in the man's face so hard, his eyes rolled up into his head and he passed out. He grabbed both women and led them out of the pub as the riot behind them grew louder.

"Reed!" Elise cried. "Oh my God! I need to go back and get him."

"I wouldn't do that," Duncan warned. "He was pretty wound up. Don't worry, a fight is exactly what he needs.

"What he needs?" Julianna cried. "Are you insane?"

"There's a rage in him, don't you feel it?" Duncan asked. "Seeing some man paw at his mate was the last straw."

Julianna looked at Elise, who suddenly went quiet. "Is he really—"

"You know why," was all Elise said.

Julianna swallowed audibly and nodded. "I know. But, maybe we should—"

"*Oi*, it's time to go!"

Turning his head toward the pub's door, he saw Finlay dragging Reed outside. Elise rushed to her mate, crying out when she saw his disheveled state and bruised face. "Reed! What the hell?"

"I'm fine," Reed slurred. "Or I will be. Ouch!" he yowled when Elise smacked him on the shoulder. "What the bloody hell was that for, woman?"

"Where's Karim and Lachlan?" Duncan asked his brother.

"Where do you think?" Finlay cocked his head back to the pub. "In the thick of it."

"Here." He tossed the car keys to Finlay, who easily caught it. "Get them home. I'll wait for those two idiots." His friend and brother were similar in that way—both loved a fight and never backed down.

Finlay frowned. "How are you planning on getting home then?"

He looked expectantly at Julianna, who rolled her eyes. "Fine, we'll wait for them," she said with a sigh.

"All right, I'll see you at home." Finlay motioned for Reed and Elise to follow him toward the Land Rover parked a few spaces down.

"Are you going to be okay?" Elise asked.

"Yeah, I'm good. Take care of him," she said, patting the other woman on the shoulder. "He needs you."

Elise nodded. "I'll see you in the morning." Before leaving though, she turned to Duncan and gave him a glare that definitely said she would do unspeakable things to certain parts of his body if Julianna didn't come back in one piece.

They watched as the Land Rover exited the parking lot, the rear headlights getting smaller until finally disappearing into the darkness.

"Is that fight still going on?" Julianna's brows drew together as shouts, curses, and loud crashes could still be heard from inside the pub.

"Looks like it."

She placed her hands on her hips and faced him. "Aren't you concerned about your brother and friend?"

"Those two?" He let out a laugh. "They got themselves into the fight, they can certainly get themselves out of it."

"Shouldn't we be calling the police?"

He scratched his head. "I s'pose someone has at this point, but Caelkirk's a small town, and stuff like this happens. Just be thankful there was no football game tonight, or we'd have a real riot."

"God! Men." She threw her hands up. "I'm going to wait in the car."

He followed her as she stalked over to the SUV. "Hey, wait a minute."

She had already climbed into the driver's seat, but before she could shut the door in his face, he held it open. "Are you going leave me out here by my lonesome?"

"All the testosterone in the air is making it hard to breathe," she fumed.

"*Och*, darlin', why are you still mad?"

"Why am I mad?" she asked. "*Why am I mad?*"

He smiled at her. "That's what I asked."

"Ugh! If it weren't for you and Reed, there wouldn't even be a fight in the first place!" She tried to shut the car door, but his hold was too strong. "What, you don't think Elise and I could handle those two creeps on our own?"

"I didn't say that." Pushing forward, his body was now between her and the door, effectively trapping her. "In fact ... you very well did show me how capable you are. I should have known you can take care of yourself."

"I—what?" Mismatched eyes grew large.

"What? I can't admit I was wrong?" He reached out and brushed the petal-soft skin of her cheek with his fingers. "Julianna, you were amazing. The way you handled that guy ... not just kicking his ass, but that you were even able to act cool and calm while he was hitting on you." Just the thought of another man touching her was making his wolf go crazy, but at the same time, he felt proud that she was so competent and skilled. "I'm sorry I underestimated you and that —*mmm!*"

Soft, plush lips pressed against his, and he ignored the

pain when the back of his head smashed into the window of the car door. Duncan wasn't sure what happened, because one moment he was apologizing for acting like a caveman, and the next, Julianna had jumped out of the driver's seat and into his arms. Well, that was unexpected, but he'd take it.

He braced her against the side of the SUV, his body pinning hers. Her delicious mouth opened to let him in, and her taste burst onto his tongue like sweet, sweet honey.

Reluctantly, he pulled away from her mouth, making her mewl. But he just had to get a whiff of her scent, so he pushed his nose into the crook of her neck. The delicious smell of cookies, ginger, and honey nearly made his brain explode.

Tracing his mouth back up to her lips, he kissed her gorgeous mouth again. Grabbing one leg, he pulled it around his waist so he could press his now-erect cock against her. Holy hell, he didn't think he could get any harder, but the way her hips ground onto him sent whatever blood he had in his body all the way to his dick. He needed her bad, and the smell of her arousal was driving him insane.

He moved a hand between them, slipping under her leggings and lower still, tracing the most direct path to its target. She moaned into his mouth when his fingers skimmed over the damp fabric of her panties.

"Julianna, darlin'," he purred against her mouth. "You do want me." Though she tried to shake her head, she gasped when his forefinger found the hardened nub of her clit. "Don't deny it."

She shuddered when his fingers pushed the wet front of her panties aside, touching her so intimately. "You're mine,

Julianna. And this"—he traced her slick lips—"is mine. I'm going to enjoy taking this sweet little pussy of yours."

"Crude bastard," Julianna growled and nipped at his lips. But from the way her pussy flooded with more of her wetness, she obviously enjoyed the dirty talk. He plunged a finger inside her, while claiming her lips once again. Her sweet cunt clasped around his finger, her hips rolling against his hand in a sweet, music-less symphony punctuated by her moans and groans.

"Beautiful." God, her smell, mixed with sex and arousal, was intoxicating. "I need you bad, darlin'."

"Duncan," she whined when he withdrew his hand. The way she said his name nearly had him losing his control like some fumbling teen. "Fuck," she whispered when he stuck his finger in his mouth to taste her.

"Like candy."

Even in the moonlight, he could see her pupils blow up with desire. He lost all sense of where they were, and all he wanted was to take her and make her his. "Inside," he growled.

Quick as lightning, she grabbed the door of the back seat and scrambled inside. He went in after her, slamming the door behind him. She lay back on the plush leather seat, her chest heaving as she took deep breaths.

Slowly, he crawled over her, grabbing her shirt and deftly unbuttoning the front. Tugging the cups of her bra down, he exposed her breasts. High and perky, they were even better than in his imagination. The large, brown nipples were already pebbled, begging for his touch. Leaning down, he took one into his mouth and sucked hard.

He licked at the hardened nipple, teasing it until she was

arching her back and her nails were digging into his shoulders. He released it and pulled her lower so he could taste her lips again while his hand fumbled with his belt. Her knees spread to accommodate him and—

"*Oi!*" *Rap, rap, rap.* "Whatcha doin' in there?"

Duncan growled as he looked up and saw his brother's face pressed up against the window. *Fucking Lachlan.* "Maybe if we stay quiet, they'll go away."

"Duncan!" A second face joined Lachlan's. Karim put his hands up to glass, cupping it around his forehead. "*Ishtar's tits!* What in the world are you two doing in there?"

Julianna let out a squeak and pushed him off her, sending him to the floor with a heavy thud. He scrambled to his knees, just in time to block Julianna from view before Karim opened the door.

"*Jaysus Christ!*" Lachlan's nostrils flared, obviously smelling the scent of sex inside the vehicle. "You gantin' so much fer it that you shagged her in the car? *For feck's sake*, you can't treat your mate—girl like all those other hens you pump!"

"We weren't having sex in here!" Julianna said defensively.

Lachlan pointed his chin down her front. "Your buttons aren't done up right, dearie."

She looked down at her crooked shirt and went red, then spun around.

"Do you need some time?" Karim asked calmly.

He scrubbed his hand down his face. "Give us a minute."

"A minute?" Lachlan cackled. "Surely you can last longer than—"

He shoved his brother away and grabbed the door, shutting it. With a deep sigh, he turned to Julianna. "You all right there, darlin'?"

"I'm *fine*." She crossed her arms over her chest.

"Hey," he put his hands up defensively. "I wasn't the one who started it—"

"*Grrr!*" She pulled the door open and slid out from the back seat. For a second, he thought she was going to run away, but instead, she walked around the front. "Get in, unless you want to walk back to the castle," she barked at Lachlan and Karim.

"Yes, ma'am!" the two replied in unison, then scrambled into the car. Lachlan climbed into the front and Duncan scooted to make space for Karim. Neither said anything, though Karim did flash him an amused smile.

The entire ride was quiet, and soon, they were pulling up to the front of the castle. She parked the car and cut off the engine, and the lights inside the car switched on.

"Julianna, may I—"

Slam! She was out of the car in seconds and making a run for the front door.

"*Och*, what did ye do now?" Lachlan asked.

"I must say," Karim began. "I am almost sorry for you. Your world must be turning upside down now that you want the one woman resistant to your charms."

"I wouldn't call her resistant," Duncan replied.

"Really?" Karim pointed his chin outside where Julianna had disappeared into the castle without so much as a backward glance. "What would you call *that* then?"

Duncan stretched his arms out, then placed his hands behind his head as he reclined back. There was no doubt that Julianna wanted him. She kissed him *first*. She was eager for his touch. Had they not been interrupted; he was pretty sure they would have taken things to the next level. Despite the interruption—and the terrible case of blue balls he was having right now—he knew things were looking up.

He grinned. "I'd call it progress."

CHAPTER SIX

When the light hit Julianna's eyes, she groaned in protest. At the moment, she would literally rather be doing anything else. Getting a root canal. Doing her taxes. Lining up at the DMV.

Literally anything else except having to go downstairs to face everyone at breakfast.

Rolling over onto her stomach, she let out a muffled moan, cringing inwardly as the events of last night flooded back into her mind.

Stupid Duncan.

It was his fault, she decided. For being the total opposite of what she initially thought him to be. Having chosen a male-dominated field, she experienced what it was like for people—men, especially—to underestimate her, particularly when she started her training with the Lycan Security Force. Being the daughter of the Alpha didn't help at all, and she had to work twice as hard to prove she deserved to be part of the training team, and even later, when she went to work for the special investigations division.

Last night, Duncan coming to rescue her like some white knight was another insult to all the hard work she'd put in over the years, but to her surprise, he actually complimented her and apologized. And not only did that make her wolf glow with pride, but she had to admit, it was pretty hot. Yes, she was weird like that.

And what happened after was even weirder. Her previous hookups had picked up on the fact that she was strong and independent, which maybe they translated to being dominant. She always seemed to give off that vibe and frankly, she wasn't into playing some submissive role and often ended up being in control all of the time. It was how she wanted it anyway—no wrong impressions, no strings attached. But then Duncan got all growly and alpha authoritative, saying the filthiest things he wanted to do to her, and *damn* if that didn't push the right buttons for her.

Those two things—stroking her pride and then taking charge of her body—was a heady, deadly combination that made her lose her mind, so much so that she would have had sex with him in the back seat of the SUV had they not been interrupted.

She told herself it was a good thing that they ended up not having sex, despite that desperate throb she felt between her legs. Even though she gave in and used her fingers to bring herself off last night, it ultimately left her feeling even more needy. She wanted to smell Duncan's masculine scent and feel his skin and his touch on her.

"Argh!" She sat up so fast that the blood rushing to her head made her dizzy. It was a good thing she was headed to England tomorrow, and she could finally leave Duncan and all this True Mates nonsense behind.

Her wolf yowled.

"Oh, shut up."

Though still feeling annoyed and reluctant, she knew she had to get up at some point and so she showered, got dressed, and headed downstairs for breakfast. Much to her surprise, there was already someone waiting at the foyer.

Prince Karim stood at the foot at the stairs looking—well, very regal, even in the casual attire of a polo shirt, sweater, and khakis. His cool blue eyes met hers as she descended, and she tamped down the urge to shiver. He was handsome, she supposed, and lots of girls would probably love to climb that tall, muscled body like a tree even if he wasn't royalty. But there was also something about him ... she couldn't quite put her finger on. Her wolf, too, was wary of Karim. It was as if under that cool composure he was keeping something big tightly wrapped up inside, like a force that could explode at any moment.

"Good morning, Julianna," he greeted.

She expected some juvenile taunt, but to his credit, he remained straight-faced and businesslike. "Good morning, Your Highness." Her eyes dropped to the carry-on bag by his feet. "Leaving already?"

"Yes, I must go today. I am just waiting to say goodbye to Duncan."

She must have winced visibly at the mention of his name because he chuckled.

"I must admit, you intrigue me." He sized her up, his eyes assessing her from head to toe so tactlessly, as only a man used to doing whatever the hell he wanted could. "A woman who is immune to Duncan's charms and doesn't immediately fall at his feet is a rare thing."

"And you, *Your Highness*?" She met his gaze head-on, unafraid, despite the fact that her heart hammered in her chest for some reason. "They don't fall at your feet by the dozen?"

"They fall for my title," he said. "But women love Duncan for who he is, not a title or his riches."

The expression on his face was practically freezing. It made her take a step back, making her bump into something solid.

"Julianna?"

That honeyed voice just went straight to her core and it took all her strength not to melt into Duncan's warm, muscled body. As if it wasn't bad enough, his arms came around her, and his scent filled her nostrils. "I, uh, was just saying goodbye to Prince Karim." Reluctantly, she took a step forward and away from him.

Duncan dropped his arms and stepped to her side to face Karim. "You really can't stay another day? Ma and Da will be disappointed to have missed you."

The prince shook his head. "Please relay to them my apologies. But I'm afraid today is the absolute last day I must leave Scotland if I am to make it back before the *Easifat*."

"The *Easifat*?" she echoed.

"Some special festival they have in Zhobghadi," Duncan supplied. "They celebrate the dust storm—"

"*Sand*storms," Karim corrected. "It's an annual event. Once the *Easifat* begins, there is no entering or leaving Zhobghadi until it ends."

"Karim has never invited me once," Duncan said in a mocked hurt tone. "And you said I was like a brother to you."

Karim chuckled, but his eyes remained cool and distant.

"It's not that kind of festival. I'm afraid it is only for citizens of my country." He looked at his watch. "I must go or my plane will lose its slot for takeoff."

"Let me see you out," Duncan said.

"I'll join you," Julianna said before she could stop herself.

The three of them walked out of the front door and into the driveway. Much to her surprise, there was an unmarked black SUV waiting outside. Two men in identical dark suits stood by the vehicle, looking foreboding.

"Wow." She pursed her lips as she eyed the bodyguards. "Where did those guys come from?"

"The *Almoravid* are everywhere and nowhere," Karim said.

"The who?" She cocked her head at him.

"Karim's personal bodyguards," Duncan explained. "They protect him wherever he goes."

"Really? Where were they last night?"

"They were there," Duncan said. "In the pub with us."

"No, they weren't," she countered. "I would have noticed if someone were following us." That was one of the skills the security force training honed in her—checking if anyone was watching or following her. "And why didn't they try to stop the fight?"

"Like I said, they are everywhere and nowhere." Karim's mouth turned up into a mysterious smile. "And they follow my orders, whatever they may be. Anyway, thank you my friend." He reached a hand out toward Duncan, his palm open.

Duncan took the hand, but instead of just clasping it, he pulled him in for a hug and said something in a low tone that

Julianna couldn't hear. A second later, they broke apart. "Safe travels, Karim."

"I wish you luck." Though he was saying it to Duncan, he was grinning at Julianna. With a nod of his head, he spun on his heel and marched toward the car. One of the guards opened the door and Karim went inside.

"What did you tell him?" she asked when the SUV had disappeared into the distance.

"I said that I considered him a brother too."

There was a sadness in his voice, and Julianna longed to comfort him. "Hey, he's not going away forever. You can see him again, right?"

"Maybe. But soon he'll be king."

"Oh." Over the last months, she'd seen a couple of news stories about the death of the King of Zhobghadi. She didn't put it together until now that he would be king soon. Duncan probably realized that once his friend was on the throne, his life would change forever, and they wouldn't just be able to spend time together as friends. "Surely he won't just forget about you. I bet you can see him again, if you give him a call."

"Thank you, Julianna."

A warm hand squeezed around hers, and she didn't realize until that moment that she had actually reached out and placed her hand in his. The urge to snatch it back was strong, but she found herself giving him a squeeze back, then gently released his hand.

"So," he began. "I saw Reed this morning. He seems to have recovered."

"From the fight or from Elise?" It was obvious the hybrid wasn't happy her mate had thrown that guy against the wall and started the fight.

"Both," he chuckled. "Anyway, last night he had mentioned he wanted to see the distillery, and so I offered them a tour today. There's some work that needs my attention, but we can leave before lunch and have a meal after."

"Sounds great." Damn, it was so hard to say no to him, especially when he turned that smile on her.

"I'll see you here at eleven then."

She was stepping aside to let him pass, but before she knew what was happening, he reached out to pull her to him. For some reason, she didn't flinch or even try to get away. Holding her breath, she imagined he would kiss her like he did last night, but his lips landed on her forehead instead. The smell of peat, malt, and pine surrounded her, and her knees turned to jelly.

Without saying another word, he walked away, whistling to himself as she stood there gawking after him. When he disappeared around the corner, she braced herself on the nearest piece of furniture she could reach—a three-legged decorative table—then let out a breath.

And that's when she realized the *third* thing about him that made her lose her mind—that vulnerable and sweet side no one else seemed to know about.

Sonofabitch.

———

"How is he doing?" Julianna asked Elise in a low voice as they sat in the back of the Land Rover. Duncan and Reed sat up front, chatting about whiskey, so she felt confident enough that neither would pay attention to them.

"Much better now." Elise rubbed her belly as she

adjusted the seatbelt. "I thought he was fine, even after we went to see his parents' graves." Reed's mother and father had been buried in the Caelkirk family cemetery, and Elise had told her they went to visit them that first day they arrived. "But I think the upcoming trip to England's got him all tied up in knots."

There was a pang in her chest as she realized they were leaving tomorrow. But, wasn't that what she wanted? She'd secured the alliance with the Caelkirk clan, and now it was time to move on and do her job. "Maybe the fight really was what he needed. To let off some steam." She herself was dreading the thought of going back to Huntington Park, though surprisingly, not as bad as she thought she would. In fact, it had been a while since she'd started feeling that dark, heaviness weighing her down.

"Are you ladies all right back there?" Reed asked, looking at them through the rearview mirror. There was no sign of the bruises or cuts on his face from last night, thanks to his Lycan healing.

"We're great," Elise said. "Are we there yet?"

"Almost," Duncan answered. "Just beyond that hill there."

"I'm looking forward to this special drink you mentioned last night," Reed said.

"Special drink?" Julianna asked.

"He claims he has a special whiskey that could get even Lycans drunk."

"What?" She raised a brow at Duncan. "Really?"

"Aye, I wouldn't lie to you, darlin'."

Did he realize that her bones just melted whenever he

turned up that accent of his? Like last night, when he said those filthy things to her and—

She cleared her throat. "And how to do you manage that?"

"We have a very special brewmaster workin' with us."

Elise leaned forward. "Special?"

"He's a—"

Julianna wasn't sure what happened, but in a split second, the entire world flipped over. She shut her eyes to stop the dizzying feeling from overcoming her, and it was only when she opened them that she realized it was she—or rather, the car—that was turned over. The seatbelt cut into her shoulders and stomach, but it was the only thing preventing her from falling on her head at the moment. Looking over to her side, she saw Elise struggling with her belt.

"Elise! Julianna!" Reed shouted. "Are you all right?"

"I'm ... it hurts ..."

An inhuman growl rattled from Reed's chest as he attempted to wrench himself free from the seatbelt.

"Duncan!" Julianna felt panic cut into her as she saw his head hanging limp. "No! Wake—"

Elise let out a scream as the vehicle turned over again, landing on the ground with a loud thud. When her brain stopped rattling in her skull, Julianna managed to unclick her seatbelt. *What the hell was going on?*

"Open it up!" a voice from the outside said. "And grab them."

As Elise's door opened, a hand came in and grabbed her. Julianna tried to go after her, but something grabbed her ankle, and she was dragged out of the vehicle.

Julianna turned to look at her attacker—and the red robe he wore told her everything she needed.

The mages.

There were seven of them, as far as she could tell. One of them held Elise, dragging her across the grass. The mage who had Julianna pushed her forward, toward where Elise was lying on the ground. She could hear the growls coming from inside the vehicle, and a second later, a full-grown Lycan burst out from the passenger side, landing on its giant paws.

"Reed!" Elise cried as one of the mages waved a hand, sending Reed's wolf flying a few feet away. She raised her arms, sending a streak of electricity to shock the mages, his body convulsing as ten thousand volts of power surged through him.

"Get her!"

Seeing her chance, Julianna forced her body to shift, pushing her wolf to the surface. Her clothes ripped as her limbs lengthened and her muscles doubled in density. Dark brown fur sprouted all over her body, covering her Lycan form head to toe. The wolf's gigantic paws barely touched the ground before it leapt into action, pouncing on top of the nearest mage it could reach.

The she-wolf opened its mouth, going straight for the mage's neck. Its massive teeth sank into fabric and skin. The mage let out a scream, but before it could bite down harder, the wolf's vision was clouded in green smoke.

A potion! Fuck! The mages had been ready.

The wolf's body went limp, its vision swimming. *Fight it,* Julianna urged. But it was no use. She could feel her limbs growing weak.

It was a good thing, however, that she had been subjected

to potions several times during her training. This particular one was probably meant to knock her out, and although it had been formulated for a Lycan, it wasn't perfect; no potion was as each recipe had to be tailor-made for the target. Soon, she would burn through it and she would regain use of her body. The best course of action was to remain still and pretend the potion was working, and then surprise them by attacking.

"Transport the bitches and the dog," a low, raspy voice said. "And kill anyone else left."

"No!" Elise was obviously still conscious, but somehow, they had managed to restrain her.

Cracking her wolf's eyes open just a fraction of an inch, Julianna could see that Elise had several lines of rope wrapped around her body. But it didn't seem like ordinary rope, as it pulsed and glowed as she moved.

"Stop struggling, my dear," the mage said. "The more you do, the more it tightens. It's magic, you see?" A few feet from her, the same rope was tied around Reed's neck as a mage held the other end, a sick smile on his face as he tugged on the rope. The wolf let out a horrific shriek.

"What ... do ... you want?" Elise gasped.

"I have particular plans for you and your mate, hybrid," he answered. "As for the other one, I bet her father and Lucas Anderson would give up anything to save her life. Even the dagger of Magus Aurelius."

"You'll never have it!" Elise spat.

"Really?" The mage laughed cruelly, and the hood on his robe fell back, revealing his bald, pale head. "We'll have to see. Maybe we'll send her back piece by piece until the dagger is ours."

Julianna wanted to rip his face off. The potion was definitely wearing off as the feeling returned to her legs and arms. They were so busy dealing with Elise and Reed that they didn't pay attention to her, but if they were smart, they'd realize that the potion they hit her with wouldn't last very long.

Think, Julianna. You're outnumbered, seven to three—

Her heart stopped. Where was Duncan?

As if he had heard her, a giant brown blur leapt out of the car and headed straight for the head mage. Duncan's wolf was huge, with thick brindle brown fur all over its humungous body. Julianna realized it was now or never, and she forced her wolf to get up and run.

A mage stepped in front of the brindle wolf, and they tangled to the ground. Another mage ran toward them, ready to throw a potion at Duncan, so she steered her wolf toward him. Her wolf's teeth sank into his arm, making him release the potion.

"Damn you! Stop them! The rope!"

No!

Her wolf was seemingly hell-bent on punishing the mage who had dared threaten Duncan that it didn't listen to her, not even when she begged it to stop and run. Something rough cut into her neck and her wolf's body was pulled back. *Fuck!*

Don't struggle! That supposedly made it worse. She heard a yowl and saw that they had Duncan too. *No!*

The mage was saying something, but she couldn't concentrate on his words because she was slowly being choked by the rope. Her wolf was struggling, unable to stay calm which only made the magical restraint tighten. Black spots were appearing in her vision, and she felt the earth move.

What?

She wasn't hallucinating. The ground *was* shaking. That stunned her wolf, and seemed to relax it enough that the rope stopped choking her.

"What the hell is happening?" The mage cried. "Who—"

The mages seemed distracted, so Julianna shifted back into her human form, then used her human hands to slip the rope off her neck. She scrambled to her feet, trying to find her bearings, but the ground swayed back and forth. She let out a gasp as the earth opened up around her, and several vines ripped up from the earth.

Vines?

No, they were tree roots! "Holy shit!"

The roots shot out toward the mages, grabbing two of them. They wrapped around their necks and snapped them, their bodies going limp instantly.

"Let's get out of here!" The mage ordered. "Now!"

The remaining three mages circled around their leader and began to chant. One root darted toward them, but it was too late. It caught only air as the mages shimmered and disappeared.

Julianna dropped to the ground when the quakes stopped. What the hell—

"Here," said a low, rough voice from behind her. She felt something wrap around her naked form—a coat. "Put this on." The accent was strange. Definitely not Scottish, but wasn't quite English.

She slipped her arms into the sleeves of the too-big trench

coat and wrapped it around her naked body—after all, all her own clothes were shredded, and she wasn't about to parade around naked. Getting to her feet, she scrambled after the man, who she realized was hovering over Duncan's prone human form.

A growl escaped her throat, and she leapt right on top of him. "Get away from him!" The man let out a surprised yelp, but she held on, wrapping her arm around his neck to cut off his airway. He sputtered and waved his hands, but she didn't let go.

"Julianna! Julianna! Stop!"

She turned her head and saw Duncan get up. "Stop!" He walked over to her. "You're hurting him."

She let out a grunt. *Well, duh.*

"He was the one who helped us!" Duncan knelt beside her. "Stop, please."

She released the man's neck, making him choke out a groan and clutch at his throat.

"That's the last time I'll try to rescue your sorry ass," the man spat as he got up. "If you weren't my boss, MacDougal, I'd have let those damn mages do what they want."

Duncan chuckled as he helped Julianna get up. "I love you, too, Soren."

Julianna grit her teeth as her wolf begged to be let out, to make sure Duncan was fine. She twisted to face him and buried her face in his neck to get a whiff of his scent.

"Calm down, darlin'," Duncan soothed as he rubbed her back. "I'm fine. Soren here got to us on time."

Her head swung over to the newcomer. He looked like an ordinary human—tall and lean, with blond hair and piercing blue eyes. But there was a power humming underneath the surface, something not even his cold, handsome face could hide. A patch of scar tissue ran up his neck and jaw, marring one cheek, making him look even more dangerous.

Warlock. And a powerful one at that, if he was the one who sent those roots after the mages.

Cold blue eyes bore into her. "What the hell do the mages want with *you*?"

"If you knew they were mages, then you probably have an idea."

He didn't flinch, but instead, cocked his head to the side. "Your friends probably need some help."

"Elise! Reed!" She had almost forgotten about them. Though she tried to run, Duncan held her tight.

"They're fine. See?"

Reed was limping toward them, an arm around Elise. "What the bloody hell was that about?"

"There could be more of them around." Soren shoved his hands into his pockets. "Let's go back to the distillery where it's safe."

CHAPTER SEVEN

Despite the fact that they were all safe inside the office of the Three Wolves Distillery, Duncan's wolf remained agitated. And frankly, he was too angry himself to contain the animal.

Those mages dare come into his territory and try to take his True Mate? The rage burned in him, fueling his need for revenge. To kill every last one of them until they were no longer a threat to his clan, his family, and Julianna.

"Here, this'll help."

He took the glass of whiskey offered to him. "Thanks, Soren. Is this batch from your special formula?"

The warlock's face remained impassive. "A very diluted portion."

Soren Shadowend was a mystery wrapped up in a puzzle, but the man was a damned good brewmaster, not to mention a powerful warlock. The Welshman had shown up on their doorstep a year ago, claiming to have a special recipe to make their whiskey potent, even to Lycans. They thought he was joking, but the warlock quickly proved he was not.

He also proved to be a useful ally. While the mages had been distracted, he quickly called the warlock on his cell for assistance. Though he had witnessed Soren use his powers to control the plants in their research lab, he'd never seen roots and trees used to attack. And frankly, he wasn't sure he wanted to see more of the warlock's capabilities.

Soren took his tray of glasses and offered one to Reed who accepted it gratefully, then offered it to everyone in the room, except for Elise. When they had heard about what happened, Callum, Kirsten, Lachlan, and Finlay immediately came to the distillery. His father, Lachlan, and Finlay were standing by the fireplace, while Elise and Reed, and Kirsten and Julianna occupied the two leather couches. Julianna had changed into some extra clothes he had in the Land Rover, and his mother had wrapped her up in one of their clan tartans. He isolated himself in the far corner of the room, as his wolf was still too keyed up.

Duncan watched as Reed took a small sip. A few seconds passed before he blinked and said, "What in the bloody hell is this?"

"Whiskey," Soren said nonchalantly.

"But ... I feel ... warm and ..." He shook his head. "It's not wearing off."

Callum laughed. "That's Soren's special formula. Our metabolisms don't burn it off quite so easily as regular alcohol."

"But how?" Reed asked.

"You're a warlock," Elise stated, her eyes narrowing at Soren. "A blessed warlock."

While there were many witches and warlocks all over the world who could make potions and cast spells, few had active powers. They were called blessed because of their additional abilities.

"And you're a hybrid," Soren stated, his eyes merely flitting on her in a disinterested manner.

"You're using magic to make alcohol stronger?" Elise's nose wrinkled.

The warlock ignored her and instead, put the tray down, leaned his hip against a large oak desk, then crossed his arms over his chest.

"Soren's first version was a wee bit potent," Callum said.

"*Wee bit*?" Lachlan exclaimed. "It knocked me out for half a day."

"It was two hours," Soren drolled.

"We've been working on a more marketable formula," Duncan added. "For Lycan consumption only, of course."

"But he's also great with the crops," Finlay said. "We haven't had such a fine harvest in the past. The stuff he grows goes into our whiskey, so I'm hoping we'll come out with a better brew in the next few years."

"You can grow plants?" Julianna asked.

"Grow plants?" Soren scoffed. "Plants grow whenever they damned well please. I merely give them suggestions."

"You can control them, then?" Elise asked.

"Something like that." He cleared his throat. "Anyway, isn't there another subject we need to talk about? Like those mages that tried to kidnap you?"

"This was why your Alpha wants an alliance, right?" Callum asked Julianna. "Those were the mages that attacked you?"

She went pale, but nodded. "It was definitely them." She

relayed what she had heard the mages say, that they wanted to bargain them for the dagger.

Duncan put the glass down, afraid it would crack in his grip. Those mages would pay for what they tried to do. It was a good thing they didn't succeed in kidnapping Julianna, because he would have torn the world apart to get her back.

"What I don't understand," Kirsten began. "Is how that mage flipped your car over. I thought mages could only use blood magic?"

Elise looked puzzled. "I never thought to ask ... but I do remember that mage who attacked Lucas and Adrianna at their first ascension ceremony. He could throw fire." She looked uncomfortably at Julianna. "Only a blessed warlock could do that."

"The mage who attacked us today used telekinesis," Reed said.

"And he was definitely a mage. His skin was a pale gray color and his eyes were red," Elise added. "From what I know from his appearance, he's already fully transformed into mage, while the others are probably partially turned."

"It takes years for a witch to fully transform into a mage, right?" Julianna asked.

"That's what I don't understand." Elise's brows crinkled. "Did mages find a way to gain power? Or take them from other blessed witches, like Stefan did?"

"No." Soren's voice was hard as steel. "The mages have been recruiting blessed witches to their side and turning them."

All the color drained from Elise's face. "How?"

"How else?" Soren shrugged. "Promises of power or wealth. Or other things."

"I can't believe blessed witches and warlocks could be bribed with things like that," Elise said incredulously.

"You'd be surprised." The warlock stretched to full height. Though his expression didn't change, his eyes turned cold, like shards of blue ice. "Of course, they have other methods of coercion."

An uncomfortable silence stretched across the room. Duncan knew the truth, of course, as did Callum, Finlay, and Lachlan. Soren came to them, not to look for a job, but for sanctuary. But that was his story to tell.

"I think what we need to do is figure out how to protect the clan," Callum said. "And prepare ourselves in case they come back."

"Good idea," Julianna said. "But you don't have to worry about the safety of your people, Alpha. The mages wanted us, and we'll be leaving in the morning—"

"What in God's name are you saying?" Duncan burst out. In a split second, he crossed the room and was looming over her. "You're not going anywhere, not while those mages are out there and they want to take you."

"Excuse me?" She shot to her feet and poked a finger in his chest. "You can't tell me what to do."

"You're my True Mate and I'll be damned if I let anything happen to you." Rage burned in his veins. *Good.*

"I have a job to do, Duncan." Her chin jutted out defiantly. "I won't be terrorized into putting my life and duty on hold because a couple of mages attacked me."

"Are you daft, woman?" He grabbed her shoulders. "They could have killed you! You could be dead and I ... No, I won't allow it."

"You won't allow it?" She shrugged his hands off. "You

can't tell me what to do. I have a duty to my clan and my Alpha. I'm headed to London tomorrow, and that's that."

"Fine! I'm going with you," he said smugly.

"What?" she cried. "You can't do that!"

"And whyever not?"

"Because ... because you're needed here!"

"My father can spare me." He looked at Callum, who gave him a nod.

"Well ..." Her eyes darted around. "You don't have permission from the Alpha of London to come to his territory."

"We've had a close alliance with the London clan for over two hundred years, and our clans travel freely between the two territories," he pointed out.

Her lips pursed together, and she looked ready to burst. And she probably would have too, had his mother not stood up and put an arm around her to pull her back down. "It's all right, Julianna. Duncan's just being overprotective. His wolf will not give him peace until it's sure the threats to you are gone. Please, let him accompany you."

She looked around, as if waiting for someone to defend her. When no one did, she crossed her arms over her chest. "Fine. I'll let you come."

As if he needed her approval. Nothing could have stopped him from going. "I'll call His Grace and tell him to expect me."

Kirsten spoke up. "Why don't we head back to the castle for some supper? Soren? Will you be joining us?"

The warlock shook his head. "Thank you, but no, Lady Caelkirk."

Soren had never been to the castle; in fact, Duncan had never even seen him leave the grounds of the distillery.

His mother brushed her hands together. "All right then, let's be off."

As they all stood up to leave the office, Duncan remained where he was, observing Julianna, who seemed to be showing her displeasure by pretending he didn't exist. But that didn't bother him. No, definitely not, not when the only thing he could think about was how, for the first time, she *didn't* deny she was his mate earlier.

Progress.

CHAPTER EIGHT

THERE WAS A SOMBER NOTE IN THE AIR AS THEY MADE their way to London. Julianna thought it was just her, but she could feel it coming from Reed and Elise too, from the moment they all met in the foyer, and until now, as they sat in the limo the Alpha of London had sent to pick them up at Heathrow. Yesterday's attack only added to the tension, but they all knew this was the day all three of them had been dreading. The heavy feeling was looming over her again, threatening to consume her.

If Duncan noticed the somber mood among them, he didn't say anything. Maybe he just thought they were all in a tense mood because of the attack. Julianna ignored him, still furious that he would come. Why did he have to be so stubborn? Didn't he realize he was putting himself in danger? Just remembering how he'd been nearly killed by the mages made that pit in her stomach grow. She didn't want to see him like that again. And she didn't want to be the cause of it. She had a target on her back, and she would be damned if anyone got hurt because of her.

"We're almost there," Duncan announced.

Reed's expression darkened, and Elise's hands gripped his tighter. Whatever she was feeling, he was probably feeling a hundred times worse. Though London looked different now than it did two hundred years ago, the countryside was pretty much the same, like the tree-lined road that led to the gates of the estate. Obviously, many things had been added and modernized, like the roundabouts they had passed, but that didn't change the feeling in the air that told her this place was familiar.

The wrought-iron gate swung open automatically as the limo drove them inside. Huntington Park was just as majestic as she remembered, like it had been frozen in time, albeit with a few differences. The flowers out front were purple, not red as they had been when they were last here. And of course, the road was paved now. The last time she had gone up this road was in a horse-drawn carriage, bumping up and down on her seat as they lumbered toward the house.

The limo stopped, and the driver came to their side to open the door. Duncan went out first. As if by silent agreement, the three remaining passengers didn't move an inch.

"At least it didn't take us three hours in a coach to get here," Julianna said wryly.

That seemed to break the tension, and Reed's shoulders relaxed. "There are some advantages to modern technology."

"Like toilets," Elise added with a wrinkle of her nose.

"Yeah, thank God. London doesn't smell like shit anymore," Julianna said, which prompted a chuckle from Elise and Reed.

Duncan popped his head into the limo. "Are you plannin' to stay in there all day?" he joked.

"Just getting our bearings." Reed exited first, then helped Elise out. Duncan held a hand out to Julianna, but she was still mad at him, so she ignored it and got out on her own.

Back in 1820, there had been an army of maids and footmen to greet them when they arrived at Huntington Park. Now, when they walked up to the front, it was a single uniformed butler who greeted them as he opened the door and let them inside.

"Duncan, glad to see you!" There was a man standing behind the butler, probably in his early thirties, with dark hair and blue eyes. "How long has it been?"

"Too long, Oliver." He took the man's offered hand.

"I was surprised when Father said you were coming as well." Oliver released his hand. "But I'm glad to see you."

Duncan nodded in agreement. "Let me introduce you to our guests. Elise, Reed, Julianna, this is Oliver Griffiths, Marquess of Wakefield and the Alpha's heir apparent."

Oliver winced at the formal titles. "It's just Oliver, please."

As they were introduced, he shook hands with Reed and Elise, but stopped when he came face-to-face with Julianna. "Have we met before? You look familiar."

"Er, your Da must be waitin' for us," Duncan said quickly. "Should we go see him?"

"Definitely. Let's go to his study."

Though the outside hadn't changed much, she could see that the interior had gone through some dramatic changes. It was inevitable, she supposed, as styles and tastes changed with the times and the different owners. They stopped outside the door that she remembered as the parlor. When they entered, she could see how much it had changed—it was more masculine, all brown leather and wood finishing, though the moldings and paneling were still all original.

The older man who sat behind the desk stood up and walked over to them. "Ah, you made it. Welcome!" His smile was bright, and based on his resemblance to Oliver, this was probably his father, the Alpha of London. As he stopped in front of them, Julianna couldn't help but notice that there was some resemblance to Reed as well. Maybe not exactly the facial features, but his air and stance reminded her of him. He shook hands with Duncan first, before turning to the others.

"This is my father, Henry Griffiths, The Duke of Huntington, and Alpha of London," Oliver began. "Allow me to introduce Mr. Reed Wakefield and his wife Elise, daughter of the San Francisco Alpha."

"Nice to meet you. Wakefield, huh? What a coincidence."

"Yes, a coincidence," Reed said without missing a beat. "Thank you for allowing us into your territory, Alpha." He bowed his head.

"Most welcome."

"And this is Ms. Julianna Anderson, sister and envoy to the Alpha of New York."

"Ah, Ms. Anderson, nice to finally meet you." He took her offered hand and shook it. "I appreciate that your Alpha thought I was important enough to send a personal envoy."

"Of course," Julianna answered. "We want to make sure you know the gravity of the situation."

Henry's expression became serious. "I've spoken with Callum, and he's relayed to me what happened yesterday.

And so—" The Alpha was interrupted by a knock on the door.

"Excuse me, Your Grace, I—oh, I didn't realize your guests had arrived." The young woman standing in the doorway glanced around the room, her sharp eyes glossing over everyone, then stopping when they landed on Duncan. "Oh. Hello, Duncan." Her ruby-painted lips curled into a smile.

Julianna felt her wolf's claws dig into her. Neither she nor her animal missed the familiar way the gorgeous blonde looked at Duncan.

"Charity, you should meet our guests." Henry motioned for her to come inside. "May I present Ms. Charity Pitt-Lane, my personal secretary, and also one of our clan members."

"How do you do?" she greeted in her posh accent. Although the Alpha introduced all of them one by one, she didn't seem interested in any of them. However, her face immediately lit up when she came up to Duncan. "It's been far too long, Duncan," she purred. "Why don't you visit more often?"

"I didn't know you'd been promoted," was all Duncan said, his lips stretched into a thin line.

She laughed and placed a hand on his arm, her fingers digging in. "I wasn't going to stay assistant secretary forever, Duncan."

The way she kept saying his name over and over again made Julianna's ears bleed, not to mention, want to tear Charity's perfectly manicured nails off each dainty finger.

"You're probably tired from your trip, Ms. Anderson," Henry began. "But if you'd like to chat now, we can iron out a few details regarding your Alpha's proposal."

"I'm not too tired, the trip wasn't too long," she said. "And the sooner we get things going, the better."

"Excellent," he said. "Charity, would you mind taking the rest of our guests to see Wadsworth? He's had their things taken up, and he can show them their rooms."

"I'd like to start my research into my family too, if that's possible," Reed said. "Anything you can do to help would be appreciated."

"Charity knows Huntington Park like the back of her hand," the Alpha said. "I'm sure she could help you with anything you need. Please assist them in any way possible."

Charity smoothed her hands down her pink, twinset jacket. "It will be my pleasure." She walked toward the door, hips swaying. "Why don't we leave them to their business and we can head upstairs?" Though she meant that for everyone, her eyes were fixed on Duncan.

"I think I'll stay," Duncan began. "I'm sure—"

"This is clan business." Oliver's tone wasn't harsh, but it was firm. "London clan business."

"And we should get it out of the way," Henry added. "I just have a few questions for Ms. Anderson. Shouldn't take too long."

Duncan looked ready to protest, but nodded in deference. "Of course, Alpha. We'll see you later."

"Let's go, shall we?" Charity's smile was bright as she waved them over, opening the door wide to let Elise and Reed through first. When Duncan walked by, she hooked her arm around his as they left.

"Ms. Anderson?" The Alpha looked at her curiously. "Shall we continue?"

Julianna uncurled her fists. "Alpha. I mean, yes. Let's get down to business."

It was a good thing she was good at compartmentalizing because she was able to box her emotions as she began her meeting with the Alpha and his son. She pretty much repeated her spiel from when she spoke to Duncan, and since Henry had already spoken to Lucas and recently, Callum, he was already agreeable to an alliance.

"We must all do our part to prevent them coming into power," Henry said. "Our clan is not as large as yours, nor do we have your resources, but we can offer our help."

"The goal is to spread the word quickly, and make it easier to call on each other in times of trouble," she said. "Plus, we want to consolidate our knowledge. Maybe someone out there knows where the last artifact is or have some idea on how we can defeat the mages once and for all."

"Maybe there's some information in the Royal Archives at the palace. I've heard they're quite extensive." Oliver said. "We could ask for access."

"The palace?" Julianna asked. "As in, *Buckingham Palace?*"

Oliver laughed. "Of course. The Royal Family knows about our existence. It's one of the reasons we've been able to keep our secret."

"You have powerful allies, too, right?" Henry pointed out.

"True." Julianna pursed her lips. "But not someone like the Queen of England. How did you manage that?"

"Over two hundred years ago, my ancestor, the Earl of Winford, served in the British Army," Henry explained. "He wasn't our Alpha, but his son was—dreadful story about the previous Alpha, we can tell you another time if you're interested—and one day, Lord Winford and his son were at a dinner where King William the fourth was honoring veterans of the Napoleonic Wars. There was an assassin present, and they saved the king by shifting into their Lycan forms."

"The crown was made aware of our existence, but only the current ruler, the Crown Prince or Princess, know the truth at any given time," Oliver continued. "So, since 1835, the London clan has been an unofficial protector of the crown. My father serves as a Royal Adviser, as does another of our clan members, the Duke of Winterbourne. We even have several members serving as personal guard to the queen."

"Wow." And Jeremy and William ... well, Eleanor and the dowager must have been so proud of them for saving the king. "That's amazing."

"Indeed." Henry leaned back in his chair. "I'll give Prince Alex a call. See what we can come up with."

"Our researchers would probably love to have access to anything they have." She got up from her seat. "Thank you, Your Grace."

"Thank you, Ms. Anderson. Now," he reached for the phone on his desk. "I have some things to attend to, but Oliver can show you to your room. We have dinner at seven, and drinks in the library at half past six."

She smiled to herself, thinking about how some things never changed, even two hundred years later. "That sounds great. Thank you, Your Grace."

"My pleasure. Oliver?"

"I'll take care of her, Father." He led her out of the study. "Have you ever been to England before?" Oliver asked as they walked down the hallway.

She bit her tongue just in time. "No, this is my first trip." *In this century.*

"It's very different from America." They turned a corner and walked toward the main foyer.

"I'm sure it is."

Oliver opened his mouth, but stopped when they heard voices coming from the end of the hall.

"... you know where to find me, Duncan." Charity sighed and placed a hand on his chest. "You know I'm always ready and willing to—"

Oliver cleared his throat to announce their presence. While Charity didn't pay them any mind, Duncan's entire body tensed when he saw them, but made no move to step away from the other she-wolf. "Done with your meeting?" he asked in a casual tone.

"Yes." Though what she really wanted to say was, *why is this bitch still touching you?* "I'm really tired, I'd love to take a nap before dinner. Oliver?"

"I'll show you to your room, of course."

As they walked by, neither Duncan nor Charity said anything, and Julianna held her head high, not minding them. Easier said than done, when all she wanted to do was rip that bitch's head off. And Duncan! He just let her grab him all over. Didn't stop her, didn't even try to conduct their intimate chat somewhere private. Nor did he mention she was his True Mate.

In fact, he hadn't mentioned it once since they got here. Not to anyone.

"Julianna?"

Oliver's concerned tone jolted her out of her thoughts. "Yes?"

"We're here."

They stood outside one of the doors in the long hallway on the upper floor of the house. She recognized it, because it had been Elise's room when they were here. Glancing down the hallway, she saw her own room a few doors down. Thank goodness she wasn't assigned there, because she wasn't sure she was ready, and today was already taxing as it is.

"Your luggage should be inside," he said. "But if you're missing anything, just use the intercom, and someone will come help you."

"Thank you, Oliver." She paused, waiting for him to leave, but he didn't budge. "Was there anything else?"

"Yes." He hesitated. "About Charity. I hope you don't think I'm overstepping, but I sensed some tension—"

"Are you going to tell me that she's harmless?" she asked in a challenging tone. "And that I shouldn't mind her?"

"Gads, no." He raked a hand through his hair. "I was going to say, don't trust her."

Now that caught her by surprise. "But she's one of your clan members."

"I can trust her when it comes to clan matters," he clarified. "However, she can be a bit ... single-minded when it comes to her goals."

And was one of her goals landing Duncan? Unless she already did. "I ... thank you, Oliver, I'll keep that in mind."

He bid her goodbye, and she walked inside, then leaned on the door as it closed behind her. Closing her eyes, she took a deep, calming breath.

Not that it worked, because all she could think about was Charity and her greedy little hands all over Duncan. Her wolf too was seething and urging her to go and wipe the floor with the bitch's face.

There was obviously some history there, and while she wasn't one to slut-shame anybody, having her own past, she couldn't help but feel ... betrayed? Used? Did Duncan really come here to protect her? Or to rekindle his romance with Charity? A seed of doubt had planted in her mind.

You don't even want him, she told herself. No, not exactly. She didn't want a True Mate and all the expectations and baggage that came with it.

"Argh!" She threw her hands up in frustration and walked over to the bed. One good thing was that at least her coming back to Huntington Park hadn't triggered that dark mood. Though she had been dreading coming here, seeing everything so different made it easier not to think of this place as it had been two hundred years ago.

She wondered how Reed and Elise were faring. Would they go see everyone's graves today? Or would they wait a bit?

A ringing sound jolted her out of her thoughts and made her reach for her phone. Checking the screen, she saw that it was time for her call with Lucas before he went to work. They had exchanged emails but hadn't really sat down to talk. She sent him a text to give her five minutes, then set up her laptop and clicked on her video call app.

The blank screen lit up as soon as the call connected, and her brother's face popped up on screen. Much to her surprise, his wife, Sofia was next to him.

"Hey, how's it going guys?"

"*How's it going, guys?*" Sofia huffed. "That's all you have to say after sending us an email saying that the mages attacked?"

Her sister-in-law's tone made her wince. "Um, sorry? I knew we were going to chat today, so I thought I'd save the story for when we were face-to-face." She looked at her brother accusingly. "Are you making Sofia do your dirty work now?"

Lucas put his hands up in surrender. "Hey, she was the one who insisted on being on this call when I told her about your email."

"I swear to God, I nearly gave birth on the spot. I had to see you were okay." Sofia exclaimed. "How are you? What happened? Everything okay? How's Elise and Reed?"

Julianna took a breath and told them everything that had happened since they arrived. Well, almost everything. She left the part about Duncan being her supposed True Mate and the painting, because frankly, she didn't think Sofia could take any more excitement. "... and you'll be happy to know that the Alpha of London has also agreed to an alliance."

"That's great news, Julianna," he said. "I knew you could do it."

"I had every faith in you," Sofia interjected. "Now, maybe you should come home and—"

"No!" That came out more forceful than she wanted it to. "I mean, I should finish our trip. The Alpha's hosting us for a few more days. It would be rude to just up and leave."

"I suppose." Lucas sighed. "We should plan out your next trips. I'm thinking we have that side of the world covered, you could go to Asia or Australia next. But"—he rose up from his seat—"I should get to the office." He leaned down and kissed Sofia on the cheek. "Daric's coming in today for a meeting, I'll definitely let him know about the Royal Archives and the Caelkirk clan's warlock friend."

She waved goodbye to her brother and was about to close the laptop down when Sofia held up a hand.

"Wait," she said. "Don't log off yet."

"What is it? Is something wrong? The baby?"

"I'm fine," Sofia said. "But, now that Lucas is gone, tell me what's bothering you."

Julianna crossed her arms over her chest. "Oh, is this an interrogation, Detective?"

Her intelligent blue-gray eyes narrowed at her. "You just seem ... I don't know. Off."

Could Sofia tell she was lying? "I'm fine."

"You know, I didn't have any brothers and sisters, but I like to think that you, Adrianna, and Isabelle are my sisters now," she began. "I hope you can tell me what's on your mind."

She knew Sofia was sincere, and frankly, she felt the same about her. But this whole thing ... she just didn't know what to say. It might take an entire day to tell Sofia about Duncan and what she was feeling right now. "I'm sorry. I just can't right now."

Sofia let out a resigned sigh. "I suppose I'm two for two with the Anderson siblings right now."

"Two for two?"

"Isabelle." Sofia's nose wrinkled. "She's acting weird. I don't know. But she won't tell me what's going on with her."

Her protective instincts flared. Maybe it was being away from her annoying sister, but if there was something wrong with Isabelle, she had to know. "What happened?"

"She's been skipping out on dinners. Sometimes she'll go missing for a few hours, and no one can track her down."

Sofia sat her chin on her palms. "She forgot she volunteered to throw me a baby shower."

"What? Oh no." She felt terrible. "I'm sorry, Sofia. Isabelle can be self-centered sometimes. Maybe she was having a bad hair day." She felt so bad for Sofia. "I'll throw you a shower when I get home," she promised.

"Really?"

She knew next to nothing about babies or showers, but she would manage. And she'd make Isabelle plan it with her after giving her a piece of her mind. "Listen, I should go."

"All right," Sofia said. "I'll let you go. But if you need to talk—"

"You're the first call I'll make."

They said their goodbyes, and Julianna shut the laptop lid. Walking over to the bed, she plopped down. There was time for a quick nap, then she would have to go downstairs and face everyone. She closed her eyes, and sleep came easily.

————

She woke up feeling disoriented, and for a moment, Julianna thought she was somewhere else.

"Jane?" she called. "Jane, is that you?"

When she opened her eyes and stared up at the canopy of her four-poster bed, it hit her. Jane was gone. Turned to dust by now. So was everyone else she had known within the walls of this grand house. Their faces flashed across her mind. Eleanor. Jeremy. The dowager. William. Rossi. Jane.

Her lungs stopped working, and her chest felt like it was

caving in. She opened her mouth, but nothing came out, not even a gasp as that gloomy feeling took over.

Hands clawed at the sheets, pulling them off as she rolled over and landed on the floor with a loud thud. Air rushed into her body, and she could breathe again.

In. Out. In. Out.

As oxygen filled her lungs, she realized where she was. And when she was.

She closed her eyes again.

Some might say she had some form of PTSD from her time travel experiences. Maybe she needed some professional help, but how could she explain to a shrink—or anyone, really —that she was feeling depressed because she met some people who had become dear to her, then they were gone in a flash?

It was silly anyway. They all lived full lives and then they died. That was how the world worked. It sucked for her that she had felt close to them, and now they were gone. But she had to move on. It's okay to miss them, Reed had said.

But some days, it was just too hard, and she couldn't let that dark, depressive feeling take over because she didn't want to lose control. It had been bad before, but today had been the worst. Even her wolf, her constant companion since she was thirteen years old, didn't know why she was feeling this way. It didn't understand why these memories were making her feel so sad. Maybe she should go home and just leave everything behind.

The alarm on her phone going off jolted her out of the deep recesses of her mind. Slowly, she got up and opened her suitcase to get ready for dinner.

A shower and fresh change of clothes had helped somewhat. Hopefully it wasn't a formal dinner, as she put on a simple pencil-cut skirt and a green silk blouse. After applying some makeup, she headed downstairs to the library, which thankfully, was still in the same place as before. The Alpha, Reed, and Elise were there, talking to a couple of people that she guessed were members of the clan. Duncan was absent, but it was early still for dinner.

"Are you all right, Julianna?" Elise asked when they found themselves alone, as the Alpha wanted to show Reed some important document.

"Huh?" Did she sense something was off? "Me? Yeah, I'm good."

The hybrid frowned. "I know it can't be easy for you. It wasn't for Reed." She glanced over at her husband. "We went to visit the graves this afternoon."

She swallowed. "How was it?" Though she didn't want to know—didn't even want to think about them—she asked anyway because that seemed polite.

"It was terrible," Elise admitted. "Reed ... he's barely keeping it together."

Julianna had no plans of visiting their graves, and she definitely wasn't going to now.

"But ultimately, I think it's good for him," Elise continued. "To start the healing process. I think ... I think you should go too."

Her heart clenched. "What? No, I'm fine," she insisted. "I don't need—"

"You've been having a hard time dealing with this too," Elise said. "Maybe you need to—"

"I said I'm fine." How did she know? Julianna clenched

her fists at her sides. This was something she had to get over by herself. Just needed some distraction and—

Her entire body went tense as Duncan entered the room. But he wasn't alone. Charity was beside him, looking like the cat that got the cream. Once again, her arm was wrapped around his, but he delicately removed it as he started walking toward them.

"Are you all right?" His eyes narrowed at her.

"I'm great," she snapped. "Good thing you found the time to join us."

He frowned. "What do you mean?"

Before she could answer, Wadsworth the butler announced that dinner was ready. She didn't bother waiting for anyone and headed straight for the dining room. However, in her haste, she bumped into Oliver.

"*Oomph*, sorry." While he wasn't as large as Duncan, he was still solid, plus the momentum caused her to stagger back. Oliver reached out and grabbed her by the waist to stop her from falling over.

"Fancy bumping into you here," he quipped.

"Ha ha." Oliver was handsome in that smooth and dashing James Bond kind of way, but he just didn't do anything for her. Maybe it was because he reminded her too much of Reed—who was like a brother to her—or maybe because he was Reed's descendant. Well, technically, Duncan was too.

"Excuse me."

Speak of the devil. Duncan was standing behind them, an inscrutable look on his face.

"Oh, sorry, looks like we're holding everyone up." He let go of Julianna, but offered her his arm. "Shall we?"

"Let's." She took his arm and allowed him to lead her into the dining room, not even glancing back at Duncan, though she could feel his gaze burning a hole in her back. Oliver sat her down near the head of the table and took the seat next to her. Reed and Elise were across from her, next to Duncan. Unfortunately, the seat beside him was empty, and of course, Charity took it.

Great. Just what she wanted. A front row seat to the Duncan and Charity show.

"*Duncan,*" Charity sunk her claws into his arm. "Do you remember that cute little bar in Brixton we went to for your birthday?"

Ah, the curtains just went up. Julianna reached for her wine glass and took a sip.

"I recall Oliver and Alan were there too," Duncan said. "And your boyfriend. What was his name? Jason? Johnson?"

She laughed, a sound that grated on Julianna's ears. "James."

Fucking how much of this did she have to endure? Taking another big gulp of wine, she concentrated on the short buzz the alcohol gave her before it burned off.

"Did you find your rooms all right?" Oliver asked.

"The room is beautiful," she said. "And very comfortable. In fact, it was so comfortable that I almost didn't wake up after my nap."

"I'm glad." He was studying her again, his brows drawing together. "I still can't put my finger on it ... why you look so familiar."

"Er, maybe I just have one of those faces?" She took another sip of wine. Did he see the painting too? Come to think of it, Duncan never told her about how Rossi's portrait ended up in Caelkirk, and she never really thought about it until now. Maybe Oliver had seen the painting when he visited Duncan. "So, what do you do, Oliver?"

As Oliver talked about his job in London at a hedge fund, she tried to listen and give her full attention to him. Of course, it was difficult, because Charity's tittering voice kept ringing in her ear, and the urge to glance over to them was too strong. The one time she did, she immediately turned her head away because Charity and Duncan's heads were bent close together, and her wolf wanted to leap out and claw the bitch's eyes out.

"That sounds fascinating," she said, almost mimicking Charity's voice.

"Really?" Oliver raised a brow. "You're interested in accelerated share repurchase in the European markets?"

Heat crept up her neck. "I ... Sorry." She took another swig of wine. "I'm an idiot."

He chuckled. "It's all right." His eyes darted across the table, then his face changed expression. "I hope you remember what I said earlier."

"About not trusting Charity?"

"Yes." He sipped on his own wine. "And don't judge Duncan too harshly."

"Don't judge ..." That pit in her stomach grew. Did Oliver confirm her suspicions about the two of them? "Duncan's none of my business."

"If you say so."

The rest of the meal passed without any more conversation from her as she concentrated on the food. Of course, it all tasted like ashes in her mouth as she could see from the corner of her eye how Charity was manipulating the conversation so only she, Duncan, and occasionally Oliver, could join, totally excluding anyone else.

Finally, the dinner was over, and Julianna wanted to shout hooray. Another moment in this dining room and she would have gone bonkers.

"How about we all head into the city for a night out after dinner?" Oliver asked as the plates were being cleared away. A few of the London wolves agreed.

"You go ahead," the Alpha said. "Show our guests a nice time out."

"Maybe one drink?" Reed looked at his wife.

"I guess an hour or two won't be bad," she said. "Julianna?"

A night away from this place and Duncan was exactly what she needed. "I'll grab my coat." It was a good excuse to leave the dining room, and she took her time going to her room to grab her purse and coat. She was coming down the stairs to wait in the foyer, but when she saw who was waiting there, she nearly turned around.

"Oh, you're coming too?" Charity said in a sweet voice.

She stiffened her spine and stopped before she reached the last step. "I was invited."

"Of course you were, Jillian."

"It's Julianna," she corrected. God help her, she never wanted to smack a bitch so much in her life.

"Anyway, you'll love the London clubs and bars, much more sophisticated than the ones in New York." Her eyes narrowed into slits. "Of course, Duncan and I won't be staying too long. We do have a *lot* of catching up to do. We didn't really spend much time *talking* today," she let out a yawn, "though I'm still exhausted." A small giggle escaped her mouth.

The meaning in her tone said it all. "How nice for you." Her wolf wanted to tear out of her and rake its claws down Charity's face. "I ... I think I forgot something." Spinning around, she ran up the stairs.

"Julianna?"

Shit. Fuckity, fuck, fuck, *shit*. Peering up, she saw Duncan and Oliver at the top of the stairs. Swallowing hard, she ran past them and headed to her room.

CHAPTER NINE

A TERRIBLE FEELING CREPT INTO DUNCAN'S STOMACH. The look on Julianna's face told him that something was wrong, and when he saw Charity at the bottom of the stairs, he knew there was trouble. His wolf snarled and clawed at him.

"What did you say to her?" He had just about had it with Charity and her damn clinginess today. Their one-night stand had happened over five years ago, and at that time, he made it clear that was all it was. Apparently, she didn't get the memo.

"Me?" Charity said with an innocent smile.

His chest rattled audibly, and because his wolf couldn't swipe its claws at her, it was shredding his insides to ribbons. "Fuck," he cursed under his breath.

"I only told her *the truth*," she purred. No doubt it was her twisted version of the truth.

"Go after her," Oliver urged.

Duncan didn't need to be told twice. He pivoted and ran.

With his Lycan speed, he caught up to her as she was entering her room.

"What the fuck—Duncan!"

He pushed her inside and slammed the door shut behind him. "Julianna," he began. But he didn't know how to continue. How to explain to her.

"Get out of my room." Her tone was careful, but there was a menacing timbre beneath it.

"Please, Julianna, let me explain—"

"You don't have to explain." She crossed her arms over her chest. "I understand what's going on here."

He raked his hands through his hair. "Whatever Charity told you—"

"I don't care about her," she said. "But do me a favor? Don't ever use protecting me as an excuse so you can come here and rekindle your affair with her."

Anger razed through veins. "Is that what she told you?"

"She said that she was 'still exhausted' from today," she spat.

He could barely keep the disgust from his voice. "Nothing happened between me and Charity today."

"Today," she huffed. "But it's true, right? You've slept with her before?"

"Aye."

Her face crumpled for a second, but she regained her composure quickly. "You're not denying it."

"I can't." He took a deep breath and took a step closer to her. "Because I won't lie to you, Julianna. I will never lie to you or keep things from you." He stared into her eyes, unflinching, willing her to believe him. "Ask me anything, and I'll tell you the truth."

There was some doubt in her face, but he could see a bit of those walls she put up crumble. "When?"

"A long time ago, right before I moved back to Scotland. It was my birthday and we were all out together. Later than night, she came to me claiming she had broken up with her boyfriend and that he hurt her." His jaw clenched at the memory of how stupid he was. Charity had been lying, of course. Both about James hitting her and them being broken up. "And ... things happened. But I never promised her anything. I made it very clear that it was a one-time thing. She agreed."

Her mouth pursed together, and he could see her shoulders relax. Another bit of that wall crumbled down. "And today? You didn't—"

"No!" He touched her arm, and she didn't flinch away. "I swear to God, I haven't touched her at all since that night."

"Then why didn't you tell me about her?" Her tone was accusatory.

"When was I supposed to? When she walked into the Alpha's study? Was I supposed to announce it to everyone?" Her expression softened. "I swear to you, I don't want her."

She cocked her head. "You certainly didn't act like it today."

"Because I was shocked. When I met her, she was just one of the junior assistants to the Alpha. I didn't know she would be at Huntington Park much less been promoted to personal secretary." His hand gripped her harder. "And I was ashamed."

Her mouth parted. "Ashamed?"

"Yes. Ashamed because of my past. Julianna, I've not been a good person. I've been with women—lots of them."

That made her flinch. "I was young and stupid, and I didn't always believe I had a True Mate. Had I known you were out there somewhere; I wouldn't have been with anyone else. But now that I've met you, things are different. You can trust that I'll never lie, and I'll always be true to you." A tightness wrapped around his chest. "But if that's not enough, then ... I understand."

"God, I hate you," she muttered.

He smiled because he didn't believe her. His hand ran up her arm, tracing a path across her collarbone, making her shiver. "And why would you say something like that?"

"Because you say ... you say the right things and it makes me want to believe you." She closed her eyes tight.

"Darlin', I meant every word." He tipped up her chin. "Open those beautiful eyes, love."

Her mouth parted, and her lids opened to reveal her gorgeous, mismatched eyes. He could see her, all of her, with no more walls between them. "Julianna."

To his surprise, she was the one who closed the last remaining distance between them. Her hands slid up his chest, wrapped around his neck and drew him down for a kiss.

He'd kissed many times in his life, but this one ... so freely given and coming from her was the sweetest kiss he'd ever received. It was also the sweetest victory he'd ever tasted. Her plush lips parted, and he slipped his tongue inside her mouth to taste her delicious mouth. Her body arched against his, the scent of her arousal unmistakable.

Slowly, step by step, he backed her toward the bed. When she didn't stop him, the tension in his chest broke, only to be replaced by lust, shooting straight to his cock and making him hard as steel. His kisses became more urgent and demanding as he pushed her down onto the soft mattress.

She moaned into his mouth when he nudged her legs apart and lifted her skirt to her waist. "You make me so hard," he whispered. "Just like this." A gasp escaped her mouth when he pressed his erection against her. "Only you, Julianna."

"*Ungh!*" She shuddered when he pushed harder, rubbing the ridge of his cock against her. Reaching down, he touched the front of her panties. "Soaked already. Tsk, tsk, tsk."

He slid down to the floor, hauling her legs down so his face was between her thighs as he knelt by the edge of the bed. "I told you I was going to enjoy taking this." He traced a finger down the damp fabric. "I only had a taste the other night. I want a whole feast."

"Will you be talking all night?" She was looking down at him, one eyebrow raised. "Well? That pussy's not gonna eat itself."

A chuckle burst from his lips. "You've sure got a dirty mouth. I know better things you can do with it later, but for now ..." He pushed her panties aside and licked a stripe up her slick folds. She cried out, her hips pushing up against him.

He steadied her with his other hand as he feasted on her sweet little cunt. She tasted even better than he'd imagined and was so wet that she was practically dripping. Her natural scent and her arousal were a heady mix, and he groaned in pain as his dick pressed up against his trousers. With a growl, he ripped off her panties so he could have better access.

She let out an indignant cry but didn't protest when he flipped her onto her stomach. He spread her thighs wider, her plump pink lips parting for him. "Delicious." He pressed a finger against her core, slipping it in, biting his lips to stop from moaning when her pussy squeezed around him. He slipped another in, thrusting it inside, and she pushed her hips at him.

Replacing his fingers with his mouth, his tongue lashed at her, tasting and devouring her as his fingers found her clit. Her hips moved in rhythm against his hand and his mouth. When her legs began to tremble, he knew she was close, and so he continued, spearing her on his tongue as his fingers pinched her clit.

"Duncan!" Her knees caved in, and her body collapsed on the mattress, her breathing heavy and uneven. God, she was gorgeous from behind, her skirt up around her waist, showing off the smooth skin and curves. As she lay there, he unclasped the back of her skirt and slipped it off, then flipped her onto her back.

Face flushed, her hair in disarray, pupils dilated in desire, she'd never looked more beautiful. As she unbuttoned her blouse and shucked it off, he did the same with his own shirt.

He shoved the straps of her black lace bra down, then cupped her naked breasts with his hands. They were perfect, just the right size for him. His thumbs caressed her already hard nipples, making her arch her back. He leaned down and took one in his mouth, rolling the hardened bud gently between his teeth.

Her hands shoved into his hair, nails biting into his scalp. It only made him bite down harder, and she bucked against him as she groaned. Reaching down, he unbuckled his belt and unzipped his fly. His cock strained against his briefs, and he shoved those down along with his trousers and took himself in his hand.

"Duncan," she gasped. "Did you bring protection?"

"Protection? From what?"

"*Condom*. If you don't, there's some in my—"

"Aye, I have one ..." He was always careful, even if Lycans didn't get diseases or could easily get anyone pregnant. Except ... "*Och*, I thought you didn't believe we were True Mates. Surely if we weren't, then—"

Her nostrils flared. "No glove, no love, MacDougal." She tried to push him off, but he caught her wrists and pinned her hands to the mattress.

Aye, she was feisty. He knew at his very being that she was his True Mate. He didn't need to prove it. While he wanted to see her pregnant with their pup, there was time enough for that later. For now ...

With a deep sigh, he let her wrists go and reached down into the pockets of his trousers, fishing for the condom in his wallet. Hopefully it wasn't too old. "Happy?" He held up the packet in front of her.

She relaxed, and so did he which was a mistake. Her leg hooked around him, and in an instant, he was on his back with her straddling him.

Mother of Mercy, he didn't think he could even be more turned on. He nearly lost control like some virgin as he looked up from under her, watching her discard her bra. She took the wrapper from him, then reached down.

"Julianna!" As her soft palm wrapped around his cock, he gripped the sheets. He tried to relax, but her hand stroking him was making it hard—er, difficult. She had a raunchy smile on her face, obviously enjoying making him squirm. "Darlin', you've made your point. I need you."

A breath escaped her mouth, and she nodded. Tearing open the foil wrapper, she slipped the sheath over him, then rose onto her knees.

"Ahh... *Fffuuck.*" His tip was barely inside her, but he wanted to burst. She sank down, exhaling a long sigh until she was fully wrapped around him. When she began to move, he thought he would lose his mind.

She was fucking magnificent with her dark hair flowing down her shoulders and those mismatched eyes boring right into him. Hot, tight, wet, and her body moved with a grace and fluidity that made her seem like she was dancing. She sheathed him, her tightness gripping his cock, and sending pleasure shooting across his brain like fireworks. Watching her beautiful breasts bounce up and down was too much, so he hauled himself up so he could taste them. *Mmm ...* When he gave a nipple a bite, she fucking growled, and that nearly made him come right then and there.

He rolled her onto her back, and she showed her displeasure at losing the upper hand by raking her nails down his back. But soon, as he fucked into her hard, she was moaning again, her hips pushing up against him.

"Come on, darlin'," he urged. "Let go." He pummeled into her, and when her tight pussy squeezed around him, he knew she was close. "That's it, Julianna. I want to feel you come."

"*Nnngg!*" she cried out as her body shuddered.

He captured her mouth, kissing her hard as their tongues danced. He held on as much as he could, loving the feel of the tremors of her body as she came again. Finally, he let go, the primal part of him howling with triumph. Unable to stop himself, he sank his teeth into the crook of her neck, then sucked the skin hard. His cock pulsed as his balls drained out, and he collapsed on top of her.

The smell of Julianna, himself, and sex permeated the room. Fuck, he would bottle that scent if he could.

She let out a small protest, and he realized he was probably crushing her. He braced himself on his elbows and looked down at her. Sweaty and glowing with that post-orgasmic buzz, she'd never looked more beautiful.

And mine.

Their eyes locked, but she didn't look away. She reached up to brush a lock of hair from his forehead, but he caught her hand and pressed his mouth to her palm. "Lovely," he whispered, before leaning down to kiss her. Softly, this time, savoring the feel of her lips. When he pulled away, she sighed but allowed him to roll onto his side and slip out of her. Reluctantly, he dashed to the bathroom to dispose of the condom, then headed back to the room.

She was still lying on the bed, stretched out like a cat. Her head turned toward him and cocked at him like an invitation. Not that he needed one, but he quickly cuddled up behind her, gathering her into his arms and holding her tight, as if afraid she was going to disappear. Nae, he wasn't going to let her go. Not now, not ever.

CHAPTER TEN

JULIANNA KNEW IT WASN'T EVEN DAWN WHEN SHE started to stir. The jet lag and the afternoon nap she took yesterday probably didn't help.

The moment that yummy, earthy smell hit her nose, she came fully awake. The warm, strong arms around her, and the rock-hard chest against her back reminded her of what transpired last night. And two more times before they both passed out.

She suppressed the chuckle rising in her chest, as she didn't want to wake Duncan. They had literally fucked themselves into exhaustion. The soreness between her legs made her wince, but then again, it was worth it. Damn, the sex had been amazing and if she had known it was going to be that way, she wouldn't have resisted this long.

Her wolf rumbled smugly.

Fine, you win. She turned around and snuggled against Duncan's chest, resisting the urge to bite his well-formed pec. He didn't stir though, and when she gave an experimental wiggle, she only got a soft snore in return. *Wow, for a Lycan, he sleeps like the dead.*

While it was nice to be in his arms, she was now wide-awake and just couldn't go back to sleep. "Duncan?" she whispered.

Nothing.

"Humph." She blew out a breath, then carefully moved his arm to his side so she could roll away. She slid her legs off the side of the bed, then turned to look at him. Hot damn, how could he be so sexy even while he slept? The sheet had fallen down low, exposing those tantalizing six-pack abs and that glorious muscled chest of his. She recalled biting that deep V on his hips more than once. With a sigh, she got up, grabbed some fresh clothes from her suitcase, and hurried to the bathroom.

After doing her business and getting refreshed, she dressed in her jeans, flannel shirt, and boots, then quietly crept out of the room. The guest wing of Huntington Park was quiet, though she did hear activity downstairs. Probably the staff getting ready for the day. Making her way down the stairs, she went out of the south exit which led to the lawn, gardens, and the rest of the vast estate.

The sky was just starting to turn pink, and the fresh cool air entered her lungs as she took a deep breath. It really was beautiful out here. A nice long walk by herself was something she couldn't do back when she first came here, since most of her days had been spent inside being taught by the severe dowager duchess of Huntington everything she needed to know to bag a husband.

A strange calm washed over her. *Huh.* There was sadness as she thought of Miranda Townsend, but also, she couldn't help chuckling at her own antics. How she enjoyed irritating the old bat. She remembered how the duchess said she wouldn't suit an Englishman, as she needed someone 'worthy of her spirit'.

Of course, her thoughts now turned to Duncan. She expected to feel more conflicted, maybe even some regret about last night. Sex for her had always been about fulfilling her needs, and while the act gave her some satisfaction, it ultimately left her feeling empty. Oh, she didn't regret her past decisions, which was another reason she ultimately couldn't stay mad at Duncan for sleeping with Charity five years ago. But all her other bed partners seemed so ... insignificant now.

Her wolf let out a pathetic sound, and she could feel its longing for Duncan. Now *that* was weird. Maybe .... maybe his whole recognizing his True Mate thing wasn't that crazy.

Her heart began to hammer against her rib cage. No, it was too early to be feeling like this, right? Last night was fucking amazing, but she can't have been dickmatized—dick hypnotized— into thinking that there was more to this than just good chemistry and sex.

A loud creak made her startle. She was standing in front of an iron gate, which had been blown open by a gust of wind. She blinked and her feet halted. How long had she been walking? And why wasn't she paying attention to where she was going?

Looking up, she saw the crest of the Duke of Huntington hanging on the gate. Blood roared in her ears, and a wave of nausea passed over her. Beyond the ornate wrought iron, she saw gravestones buried in the grass. How the hell did she wind up here? Her hand trembled as she reached for the gate, then pushed it open.

Sunrise in a graveyard would have brought chills to anyone, but the reverent silence that hung in the air amongst the gravestones was almost soothing. Most of the older ones were barely readable, but as she continued to walk, the newer ones were still clear. A group of marble stones near the corner made her stop, and her knees buckled.

And so, they were all here together, their individual headstones engraved with dates and their names.

Miranda Georgiana Townsend, Duchess of Huntington
Eleanor Abigail Charlotte Griffiths, Countess of Winford
Jeremy Augustus Frederick Griffiths, Earl of Winford
William Lowell Richard Griffiths, Duke of Huntington

Julianna didn't even realize she had been crying until the taste of salt touched her lips. Her heart wrenched thinking about them, and a sob ripped from her throat. Her entire life, she'd really only lost one person—her Nonna Gianna, who had died of old age. Standing here, it hit her like a sack of bricks that she lost *all* these people in the blink of an eye.

And it seemed so trivial, because she'd only known them two weeks. But how could she forget little William's charming antics? Or the way Eleanor welcomed them when they arrived in that strange world and she was scared out of her mind? And Jeremy and his warmth, and the way he acted like a protective older brother to her and Elise?

And the dowager duchess. Oh, how she hated the old hag in the beginning. But Miranda Townsend challenged her and made her want to be better at everything. Made her boring life more exciting, and in the end, told her she had been so proud of Julianna most of all. It couldn't have been easy for the dowager losing her son and grandson a year apart. Her heart ached for the old woman, who, based on the date of death on her gravestone, hung on for another forty years, probably to irritate her great-grandchildren.

Her choked cries turned to laughter. Laughter at all the amazing experiences she had in the past. It was still mind-boggling, and if it wasn't for that gorgeous silk gown hanging in her closet back home in New York, the one she had arrived in when they traveled back to the present, she would have thought she had dreamt it all.

With a deep breath, she straightened her spine and wiped the tears from her face with the sleeve of her shirt. There was a sadness lingering in her mind and in her heart, but there was also a sense of ... relief? Like she had been carrying this great weight around with her for months and months, and while it wasn't totally gone, she could feel the load had lightened. She cleared her mind and said a small prayer for everyone from the past, including those who weren't buried here.

By the time she walked out of the cemetery, the sun had risen, bathing the land around her in early morning light. She could see the house in the distance and then realized just how far she had walked.

"Julianna?"

She turned her head toward the sound of the low, smooth-as-honey voice. Warmth curled in her chest as she saw Duncan walking up the path toward her. Dressed in a loose white shirt, dark pants, and boots, he looked like he himself had stepped out of the 1800s.

"Duncan?"

"I've been looking all over for you." He rushed at her,

hands gripping her arms. "Where were you?" he growled, his dark blond brows slashing downwards in anger. "You left without—" His face changed in an instant. "Have you been crying darlin'?"

"No—"

"Don't lie." His tone had softened, but there was a raspy quality that made her shiver. "I can see you've been crying. What's the matter?"

She swallowed hard. "I ... I can't ... not right now, please, Duncan?" What was she supposed to tell him? She couldn't lie to him, not anymore.

A sense of dread passed over her. He vowed that he would never lie to her, but how about her? How could she tell him about the past and—dammit—that painting. That it was *her* in the painting.

"Do you regret last night?" he asked, his jaw tensing.

"No!"

"Then what's wrong?" He shook her gently. "Tell me, please."

Her breath caught in her throat, and her chest wanted to burst, wanted to tell her secret. But it wasn't just her secret to tell. She had to think of Reed and Elise. And the safety of her kind, because if the mages figured out what that dagger could do ...

He loosened his grip. "I see you're not ready to share this part of you yet," he began. "But soon I'll know everything about you." He leaned down and pressed a warm kiss to her forehead. "Why did you leave the bed this morning?"

"Jet lag." She leaned into him, allowing his scent to tickle her nostrils. "Couldn't go back to sleep."

"And you didn't think to wake me? I could have found

better ways to spend the morning than going to an old grave-yard," he said, his tone lightening.

"A nuclear explosion couldn't have woken you up."

A chuckle burst from his mouth. "*Och,* you'd done and worn me out, you minx. But then I know you wanted me so bad and could not get enough."

She snorted.

"I have scratches on my back and arms to prove it."

"And I have matching bruises on my thighs and ass." When Duncan marked her, her wolf loved it so much that it urged her to do the same, preferably somewhere visible. Possessive little bitch.

"Really? Can I see?" An impish smile formed on his mouth as he tugged at her jeans.

She pushed his hands away and smirked at him. "I'm not getting naked in a graveyard."

"We're outside the graveyard, darlin'." He rubbed his chin with his thumb. "I do have an idea. Why don't we go for a run with our wolves? Mine's been dying to spend time with your she-wolf."

"Wait, out here? Is it safe?"

"There's acres and acres of land around here. No one will bother us. I used to run around by myself whenever I visited. Never saw a single soul." He was already unbuttoning his shirt. "C'mon."

Her wolf really loved that idea and went giddy with anticipation. "All right."

They walked off the path, into the line of trees so they could remove their clothes and hang them up in a branch to keep them safe. Duncan licked his lips as his gaze boldly raked over her naked body. The rush of wetness to her pussy tinged the air with arousal and she couldn't help but notice his cock was half hard.

"Last one to shift's a rotten egg!" She darted off into the trees, and began to let her wolf take over. The rush of a shift was always something she looked forward to. As part of her training, she had to learn to shift back and forth as fast as possible, something that came in handy the other day. It did now too, as she heard Duncan's indignant shout as he tried to chase her.

Her wolf's body allowed her to run faster than most creatures in the world. However, when she heard the thunderous sound of paws hitting the ground, she knew she was about to be matched. She pushed her animal faster, but Duncan's brindle brown wolf caught up to her. Side-by-side, they roamed to their hearts content, occasionally nipping and teasing each other.

She wasn't sure how long they were running, but at one point, Duncan's wolf was leading her. Her wolf was getting tired, so she was falling behind, and though he slowed down, he remained ahead, his wolf cocking its head as if telling her to follow. Not really sure where they were going, she followed him, until they came to a clearing where there was a large, manicured hedge. He continued forward, and her wolf slowed to a trot as they stopped in front of a small metal gate hidden within the shrubs. *What was this place?*

The brindle wolf began to shrink, and its fur sank into skin. Getting up from his crouched position, Duncan opened the gate and then waved her in.

Her wolf was wary of this unfamiliar territory, not sure ... there was something familiar in the air. It walked forward, into the middle of this strange place and stopped beside Duncan.

"Hey, pretty wolf." Duncan knelt down and scratched the she-wolf's head. The wolf responded by jumping at him and licking his face. "*Och*, you're just as feisty as Julianna." He gave it a good rub down its neck and flank. "I love playin' with you, but d'you think I can have her back now?"

Julianna felt the she-wolf withdraw back into her body, and soon, she was sitting on the grass next to him. "Where are we?" As Duncan helped her up, she blinked, looking around at the large, white blobs of stone around them.

"It a secret place." He reached out and plucked a leaf stuck in her hair. "Only the family knows about this secret statuary, but Oliver told me about it and how to find it. I've never actually been here though."

"It's like a garden, but with statues." The sculptures were scattered around the enclosed garden, and were different sizes. Some were life-size while the smaller ones were placed on pedestals so it was easier to look at. She peered at the closest one of two figures kneeling. *Weird.* The figures looked like— "What the hell?" Upon closer inspection, it was a sculpture of a man and woman, partially naked as her top was pulled down to bare her breasts, while the man sucked on a nipple and had a hand under her skirt.

"It's an erotic statuary," Duncan said with a chuckle.

"I can see that," she said wryly. There were many other couples around them, frozen in marble, stone, and bronze in varying positions and poses. She stepped back and nearly collided into a life-sized statue of a man lifting a woman up in his arms while impaling her on his cock.

Duncan nodded at the one beside him. It was of a woman

tied up against a column, head thrown back in ecstasy, while her lover was on his knees in front of her, face buried between her legs. "I think this one's my favorite." His eyes dropped down to the same place between Julianna's legs, and she felt heat rush to her stomach.

"Is there a reason you brought me here?" Not that she needed to ask. She already knew. Damn horny fucker. Of course, she wasn't much better.

"Well, I've always wanted to see this place." He looked around as he walked toward her, his eyes lingering on a statue of a woman on her knees, mouth on a man's enormous penis. "It's not as explicit as the stuff we have on the Internet now, but I imagine over a hundred years ago, this was shocking."

He was moving closer, and she found herself backing away, the heat and tension growing between them. She wondered if she ran, would he chase after her? The blazing twin green fires of his eyes said yes. But she didn't find out because she bumped into something solid—hard, smooth stone pressed on her naked back, and when she looked up, she saw a life-sized statue of a naked, busty woman splayed down, her legs spread as she touched herself.

"Julianna," he rasped. Reaching toward her, he touched her on the arm sending a tingle down her spine. His fingers traced up to her shoulder.

"Duncan, we don't ... you can't—" She gasped when his large hand collared her throat; not choking her, but enough to keep her in place.

"Don't tell me what I can and can't do," he growled. "Your sweet little body is mine."

"Ha!" She tried to twist her head away, but his grip tightened.

"You don't believe me? Let me show you."

Holy shit, that display of dominance should have had her knocking him flat on his ass, but instead it made her pussy wetter than the Atlantic. He must have smelled it, because he pushed her up against the marble slab, trapping her with his body. His cock, now fully hard and engorged, pressed against her stomach. She opened her mouth to protest, but he covered it with his in a rough, hard kiss.

She moved her hands down wanting to touch his cock, but he caught her before she got too far.

He pulled away, a wicked smile on his face. "I didn't say you could do that, did I?" He raised her arms above her head, and made her grasp the stone statue. "Now, I don't have any rope to tie you with, so you'll have to keep your hands here. Don't move, or I'll spank your bottom red."

Fuck, she wondered how that would feel, to have his hand smack down on her ass. Just thinking about it made her shiver.

"Oh, you think you'll like that, huh?" He nipped at her earlobe. "Maybe another time. Your pussy smells incredible, and I need to taste it again." A trail of fire was left in the wake of his mouth as he made his way lower. He was on his knees in front of her, eyes like glittering emeralds as he looked up at her.

"Fuck!"

He wasn't gentle or subtle as he licked and sucked at her pussy, nor did he look away from her. Those emerald eyes stared up at her as he ate her out, his tongue and lips doing wicked, dirty things to her. She wanted to reach down and tug at his hair, but kept her hands in place as he'd ordered.

Pleasure spread through her, building in intensity as he continued to tease her.

"Duncan!" She gripped the marble stone but quickly released it in case it crumbled in her hands. Her orgasm ripped through her, her body shaking. And Duncan, damn him, didn't stop, not until his wicked, talented tongue coaxed another orgasm from her.

"Please," she moaned, letting her hands fall to his shoulders. "I can't ..."

She was spun around to face the statue, her naked, overheated body pressed up against cold marble. "What did I say?" he tsked. "I said to keep your hands above you. And you disobeyed me. You know what that means."

A hand smacked her on the ass, making her jump. The stinging pain was quickly soothed away by his warm palm rubbing the flesh. "You're asking for it, aren't you, Julianna."

"No." *Yes.*

"Don't lie, darlin'. Or there'll be more where that came from."

Fuck, that thick honeyed voice of his made her knees weak, and she had to hold on tight to the marble statue to stop herself from sliding to the ground.

"Now, keep those hands in place." He leaned forward, so that his chest was pressed up to her, and his thick, hard cock brushed against her ass. A hand snaked down between her legs, and, *motherfucker*, her thighs automatically spread to give him easier access.

"So wet and ready for me, my Julianna. You came so hard, like a good girl." A finger stroked up and down her wet lips, while his thumb found her clit. "You want me so bad.

Want me to make you come over and over again with my cock inside you."

"D-D-Duncan." She sounded pathetic and desperate. She didn't care.

His head bent down, opening his mouth so he could graze the skin of her neck with his teeth. "I bet you want it so much, you'd let me fuck you right now, even without a condom."

Her entire body froze, fear gripping her. Or maybe it wasn't fear. Maybe it was excitement. "I—" Her eyes rolled back as his finger entered her roughly, moving in and out as his hips nudged her, his cock smearing pre-cum on her ass.

"This is mine now, Julianna. Your pussy, your sweet body. All of it. I'll have you without any barriers. Fuck you raw and fill you with my cum."

And in that moment, she wanted it too. She pushed up against his hand, her body shuddering as his digits worked her harder.

"But not now." Irritatingly, disappointment flooded her. "Because, darlin'"—he nipped at her shoulder—"I won't just settle for your body. I want it all." He plunged another finger into her. And then another. And, goddamn him, she did want his cock inside her right this moment. Even if it meant ...

She cried out when he pulled his hand away before she could come again. Something butted up against her thighs—his cock, based on the thickness. He slid his cock between her thighs, already slick with her wetness. Oh God ... it was fucking hot. Looking down, she saw the tip of his engorged penis peeking from between the front of her thighs, sliding in and out.

"Oh!" Fucking hell, he drove his shaft against the seam of

her pussy, riding along her clit. Was he really going to do this?

"Keep those thighs pressed tight, darlin'," he whispered, his breath hot in her ear.

His shaft continued to slide against her, rubbing her in all the right places. It was dirty and depraved, and the fact that all she had to do was angle her hips a certain way and he'd be inside her thrilled the hell out of her.

"So. Fucking. Good." Duncan groaned. He reached around to cup her breast and give himself more leverage to thrust harder.

"Fuck!" She pushed her hips back at him, enjoying the feel of his cock as it slid in and out of her thighs, the tip hitting her clit at just the right angle. His thrusts became faster, and though her knees were starting to feel stiff, she ignored it as her body began to tighten, waiting for the orgasm she knew was coming. When he pinched her nipples and then leaned down to sink his teeth into her neck, deep enough to leave a mark and suck at her skin, her body exploded.

His cock pulsed between her thighs, and his cum burst from the tip, coating her stomach with his seed, while some splashed on the white marble. A grunt escaped his mouth as he pushed forward one last time before pulling back.

They stood like that for a few more seconds before Duncan flipped her around to kiss her hard on the mouth. "Good girl," he said against her lips, and damn if the way the *r* tapped off his tongue didn't make her pussy thrum with desire. Despite the three orgasms she'd had, she still felt unsatisfied and empty without him inside her. "We should go back."

"Yes," she panted against him. Back in her room, where she had at least one more condom in her suitcase from her travel stash. "I—"

They both froze at the sound of metal screeching against metal. Someone was opening the gate.

Duncan moved so fast she went dizzy. He grabbed her arms and moved her to the other side of the statue where the intruders wouldn't be able to spot them. When he put his fingers to his lips, she nodded.

"... are you sure you lost it here?"

"I haven't seen it since we got back last night," came the answer. "It was in my coat pocket."

"So maybe it dropped to the ground when you took it off, Reed?"

Julianna frowned up at him. *Reed and Elise?* The expression on his face told her he was just as confused.

Maybe if they kept quiet, the other couple would eventually go away.

"I ... hold on. There's someone else here."

Oh fuck, they sensed us. When she saw Duncan open his big fat mouth, she shook her head. But it was too late.

"Oi, what're you two doing here?" he shouted from behind the marble as he craned his neck.

"What the—Duncan?" came Reed's reply. "What are *we* doing here? What about you?"

"Just ... you know, went out for a run. Er, you and Elise should probably stay where you are, unless you're wanting a free strip show." She punched him on the shoulder. "Ow! *Fer feck's sake*, Julianna, d'you want them to see you naked as the day you were born?"

"Julianna?" Elise's voice was filled with amusement and Julianna groaned. "Are you—"

"Yes, I'm here." She raised a hand high and waved even though she couldn't see them.

"Oh. Right." Reed cleared his throat. "Apologies for the interruption."

"That's all right, we just finished. Ow! Julianna, keep your claws to yourself."

"Just keep your mouth shut," she hissed.

"It's too late, darlin'," he cooed. "They already know what we were doin' here." His brow wrinkled. "We went for a run this morning, hence our current state of nakedness. Say, how did you guys get all the way here?"

"We rode in on horseback," Elise explained. "Er, we're really sorry, we didn't think anyone would be out here this early. Reed can't find his phone. He thinks he dropped it here last night."

Duncan's brow furrowed further. "Wait a minute, what do you mean 'dropped it here last night'?"

"Er, Reed couldn't sleep after we came back from the bar," Elise said with a nervous laugh. "So, we went for a ride and came here."

"How did you know about this place?" Duncan asked. "I was told only the Alpha and Oliver knew this existed."

"You know what?" Reed said. "My phone isn't really important; I can buy another one. We'll head back."

"Wait—"

"Bye!" Elise shouted. "We'll see you later."

The sound of the gate closing indicated that the other couple did indeed leave.

"Why did you have to go and do that?" Julianna hissed.

"Do what?"

"Tell them ... I mean ... that we ..."

He chuckled and kissed her nose. "*Och*, darlin'—first of all, we're standing here naked as jaybirds; I think they would have noticed us. And"—he gave her a heavy-lidded gaze—"if you think I'm keeping what's happened between us a secret, you've got another think comin'. I would shout it to the world if I could."

"You wouldn't."

"You wanna try me?" When she smirked, he flashed her a smile, stepped back and opened his arms wide. "Helloooo world!" He spun around. "Know that I, Duncan MacDougal, have finally succeeded in getting Julianna—"

"Stop!" She launched herself at him. "Stop, you lunatic!"

He caught her and twirled her around. "Aye, I'm a lunatic. Loony for you, darlin'."

A warmth bloomed in her chest, and though that practical side of her wanted to squash it away, she set it aside for a moment. Just for now, just for this morning, she would just let things be and not ruin them. "Crazy." She gave him a peck on the cheek. "C'mon, lets shift and head back. I need breakfast."

"Whatever you want."

As they walked hand in hand back to the entrance, Duncan halted, then frowned. Bending down, he picked something up from the ground. "Well, fuck me, here's his phone."

"Sounds like we aren't the only ones making good use of this place." She shook her head, not wanting that mental image of Reed and Elise doing ... well, the same thing she and Duncan were doing out here.

"I don't think Oliver would have told them about this place." Duncan stared at the phone. "He made me swear on my grandmother's grave not to tell anyone I knew about it. And we've known each other since we were in short pants."

Oh Christ. Reed probably knew this place because he'd once been the Duke of Huntington. "Er, maybe they went exploring last night?" That sounded pathetic even to her, and she could tell Duncan wasn't buying it either. Would he put two and two together somehow? "Anyway, it doesn't matter." She slid her hands up his chest. "What are we dilly-dallying around for anyway? I want food. And bed."

His brow shot up. "Is that so? Well, I can't keep a lady waiting now."

———

After shifting back to their wolf forms and retrieving their clothing, they snuck back into the house. Though Duncan tried to drag her back upstairs, she wanted to have breakfast, so they headed to the informal dining room.

The Alpha, Oliver, Elise, and Reed were already seated at the table. As they entered, Oliver's brows rose at their linked hands but he said nothing. She sighed inwardly. It wasn't like they could hide anything, not when everyone saw Duncan go after her last night and then they didn't come down to join them for their excursion to London.

"Good morning, Alpha," Duncan greeted as he pulled a chair out for Julianna.

"Good morning, Duncan. Julianna," Henry looked up from his newspaper. "Sleep well?"

Oliver guffawed, but covered his mouth with a napkin.

"Yes, very well." He reached for a plate of eggs and piled some on Julianna's plate.

"Now that you're all here, I have some exciting news." Henry put his newspaper down. "We have a special guest tonight. None other than His Royal Highness, Prince Alex."

"*The* Prince Alex?" Elise looked confused. "Of Wales?"

"Yes, the Crown Prince himself," Henry said. "As I promised, I told him that you wanted access to the archives. When he heard that we had Lycan visitors from America, he asked to meet you all."

"Wait, the Prince knows about Lycans?" Reed asked.

Oliver nodded. "They do." He relayed the story Julianna had heard the day before about Jeremy and William and how the Crown now knew about Lycans. She couldn't help but notice Elise and Reed look at each other warmly when they found out what happened, and it was hard to stop from smiling herself.

"I'm a wee bit cross, because I'm not the one putting that smile on your face," Duncan whispered in a low voice. "But I can forgive you because you look absolutely beautiful with it."

If she were the type to blush, she probably would have. Instead, she rolled her eyes at him. "Does that work with every girl?"

He grinned. "I can see you're still not going to make this easy for me."

"Should I?"

"That's okay," he leaned down and bent his head to hers. "I love it when you're feisty. Because I know later on, you'll be screamin' my name again when I get on my knees and feast on you."

Heat crept up her cheeks, and she suspected they were as red as a fire engine. *Damn him!*

Henry stood up, folded his paper, and tucked it under his arm. "I have a busy day, especially with tonight's dinner, so I'll leave you young ones for now. Oliver, perhaps you can entertain our guests?"

"Of course, Father."

"Excellent. Have a good day then." He walked out of the dining room, leaving the rest of them behind.

"So," Oliver began, the corners of his mouth turning up as he turned his gaze toward Julianna and Duncan. "We missed you last night. I thought you were joining us?"

"We had other plans," Duncan said smugly.

"I'm happy for you both." Oliver laughed when Julianna gaped at him. "Don't look surprised. I suspected something was up when Duncan showed up at the last minute. She's yours?"

"Aye," Duncan nodded, prompting Julianna to roll her eyes again. "But she doesn't believe me still."

"He hasn't won your heart yet?" Oliver asked Julianna.

"There's nothing to be won," she replied wryly. "I'm not a prize."

"Yes, you are." The heat of Duncan's stare could have made her burst into flames on the spot. "The only prize worth winning."

Dammit, when he said things like that and gave her one of his goofy smiles, it made her heart melt. *Stop!* She clenched her jaw. *I only want him for his talented tongue and the mind-blowing sex,* she reminded herself.

"Make her coffee, she'll propose marriage," Elise piped in.

"What?" Duncan's fist landed on the table, making the teacup clatter loudly against the saucer.

"It was *coffee*," she said. "Hot and fresh, right when I needed it. I would have proposed marriage to anyone who brought me food at that point."

Back when they first arrived in 1820, Cross, who had the power to change the form of matter, "made" them fresh hot coffee from thin air. After an uncomfortable night on a sleeping bag in a musty old house, seeing the hot brew nearly made her weep, and she joked that Cross should marry her.

"And exactly *how* many men have you proposed marriage to?"

Duncan was red, all the way to the tips of his ears. It was adorable, which is why she gambled and asked him sweetly, "This week?"

"Woman, you're really askin' for it."

She sighed. "For God's sake, that was a joke."

"But you also said Cross was hot," Elise added.

Jesus, did she have some sort of death wish? "I wasn't—"

"I'm going to kill this Cross." Duncan threw his napkin on the table. "You're my True Mate and—"

"Can it with caveman act, will you?" She grabbed the basket of bread and took a slice, biting into it. "He's nobody, okay? He works for the clan, just like I do and ..." Shit, how was she going to explain it? "We had a mission, and he made me coffee when I woke up."

"When you *woke up*? Like from *bed*?" Steam was practically coming out from his ears.

"It was the floor, actually." Okay, she had to admit, that made it sound worse. But she couldn't help but feel a *tiny* flare of satisfaction at his reaction. "Look, it was a top-secret mission from our

Alpha. Cross left Elise and I alone to investigate something, and it took him a while to come back. When he did, he made—yes, made it, because that's one of his powers—coffee for me *and* Elise." She glared at the woman in question, who seemed to be trying to hide her amusement behind Reed's shoulder.

That seemed to calm Duncan enough so he could sit back down on the chair. "No more proposin' marriage, you ken?" As if to prove his point, he snaked a hand around her head and pulled her in for a hard kiss.

"Fine, I promise I won't propose to any man," she said wryly. "Happy?"

"For now."

Oliver cleared his throat. "If we're done with marriage proposals and murder threats, perhaps we could go for a tour of Huntington Park?"

"As long as it doesn't take too long." Duncan placed a hand on Julianna's thigh, the warmth making electricity zing across her skin. "We'll be busy." She glared at Duncan, but he gripped her harder. When his nostrils flared, she knew he could smell how her panties drenched, and his frown turned into a grin.

"I'm sure you will be," Oliver said dryly.

After they all finished breakfast, Oliver did take them on a tour of the house and the gardens. Julianna marveled at how different yet the same everything was. Many of the rooms still had the original paneling and moldings, but the furniture and decor were different and modern. She could see how the following owners of the house had obviously taken care of Huntington Park, and she was glad. Based on the look on Reed's face, he was too.

It was strange, really; her stomach was all in knots at the prospect of coming here, but now she wondered why. Sure, there was a touch of sadness, but the fond memories made her smile.

When they had gone from top to bottom of the house, the tour finished in the formal sitting room with high tea.

"Oh my God." Julianna's eyes devoured the spread of pastries, savories, cakes, and of course, scones with clotted cream and jam. "I swear, this is one thing the English do right." Really, this was the only reason she'd endured the dowager duchess's "lessons", so she could have all the delicious food during teatime. Until this day, she still couldn't find scones, pastries, or even butter that tasted as good as it did in the 1800s, perhaps because today's food was all made with preservatives and fillers.

They all sat down with Oliver, Reed, and Elise occupying the three wing chairs and Duncan deftly steering her to sit with him on the love seat. Not that she could get away, because he kept his fingers threaded through hers the entire day. His small touches here and there, deliberate or not, surprisingly, didn't annoy her. She found herself wanting to touch him all the time too.

"These are amazing," Julianna declared as she popped a mini salmon sandwich into her mouth. "Hmm ..."

"I love a woman who can eat." Duncan's eyes gleamed as she licked a stray bit of cream cheese from her lips.

"Really? Then pass me those scones."

He did, placing two of them on her plate and then holding the tray with the jam and clotted cream so she could pile her scone with them, then take a large bite. "Hmm ..."

Now these were almost as good as she had had over two hundred years ago.

"Excuse me, Lord Wakefield, apologies for interrupting your teatime."

Julianna's hackles rose as her eyes snapped open. The bite of scone nearly choked her when she forcefully swallowed it down.

Of course, *she* was still lurking around Huntington Park. *Tramp*. Charity was looking gorgeous as ever, her blonde hair up in a sleek French twist, wearing a powder blue tweed suit and matching shoes. As usual, her eyes zeroed in on Duncan, even as she addressed the room. "I just wanted to remind everyone of tonight's dinner. Prince Alex will be arriving at seven thirty and we shall all be expected to welcome him in the foyer."

To his credit, Duncan didn't even turn toward her. Indeed, he seemed to be busy, delicately piling a plate with cakes. When he was done, he offered it to Julianna. "Try these, darlin', they're delicious."

Charity cleared her throat. "I do hope everyone here can be appropriately attired, as it will be a formal dinner." Her gaze narrowed on Julianna, her eyes drifting down briefly to the crumbs all over the front of her sweater. She gave an exaggerated shudder. "Of course, if *anyone* feels they aren't up to snuff with their table manners, feel free to sit this one out."

The remaining piece of scone in Julianna's hand crumbled as her hands tightened into fists.

"Duncan," Charity began, "I was thinking we could—"

"Aren't you adorable?" Duncan reached out, brushed the corner of her mouth with his thumb, and showed her the bit of cream on the tip before licking at it. "Delicious." A low growl vibrated from his chest. The sexual energy could have set the entire room on fire. It made her temporarily forget that she wanted to rip the other woman's pretty blonde scalp from her head.

Charity, on the other hand, let out a small indignant squeak, then opened her mouth. "Dun—"

"Thank you, Charity, that will be all," Oliver said, effectively dismissing her. "I'll see you later tonight."

The blonde's set face, fixed eyes, and clamped mouth made Julianna want to raise her arm in triumph. Charity gave them a curt nod, turned on her heel, and left.

Duncan brushed away the crumbs in her hand, then calmly handed her a fresh, warm scone from the basket on the table. "Have another, darlin', that one seemed a wee bit dry."

His mouth was quirked up into a smile, and she wanted to kiss him right then and there. If she had any suspicions that Duncan still wanted Charity, they had been immediately and effectively crushed. He hadn't acknowledged her, not even looked at her the entire time she was in the room.

Still, as she bit into her new scone, Julianna couldn't help the irritation that was beginning to gnaw at her. While Duncan was definitely sending the message that he was not playing her games, Charity didn't get the news. She might try something later on, so Julianna knew she had to be prepared.

Tonight was her chance to make sure the assistant backed off. A good physical smacking down would send a clear message, but maybe there were other ways to keep the hussy away. *Hmmm. Maybe the duchess's lessons weren't going to be useless after all.*

CHAPTER ELEVEN

Duncan was glad he had brought his kilt along, not just because of the impromptu dinner with Prince Alex of Wales, but also because of the way Julianna's eyes darkened with desire when she came out of the bathroom and saw him in his formal Scottish wear.

"If I show you mine, will you show me yours?" His eyes roamed the curves of her body, wrapped up in a sinfully red dress that showed off her shoulders and a hint of cleavage. When she stepped forward, his mouth went dry when the skirt parted, exposing the length of a long, slim leg. A leg that, not more than an hour ago, had been wrapped around his waist. Now, however, thinking about her going downstairs in that thing made him want to throw a blanket over her. "D'you think maybe your dress is broken, darlin'?"

"It's my stupid sister," she moaned. "Adrianna put this dress in my suitcase without telling me, and I didn't realize the slit would be cut up to Alaska."

"Maybe you can get another dress. I'll buy you any dress you want." Preferably one that covered her head to toe.

She harrumphed. "Well, if *someone* didn't want to spend the afternoon in bed, then maybe I would have had time to go out and get a new one."

"*Och*, I didn't hear you protestin' too hard now," he reminded her. Nor did she protest when he got his suitcase from his room and brought it here, telling her it would save the housekeeping staff time to make up one less room a day.

"This is my last clean dress and the only formal wear I have." Using her palm, she smoothed back her hair, which was pulled up into an elegant twist. "I wasn't prepared to dine with royalty."

He longed to release her glorious dark locks from its confines, to watch it tumble down her shoulders and back, but then again, an unreasonable flicker of jealousy made him want to keep the sight of her hair unbound to himself. "It's beautiful. You're beautiful. You've nothing to be worried about."

A small line of worry formed between her brows. "Have you met him before?"

"The Prince?" He shook his head. "I know all about the history of the London clan and the royal family, of course, but I don't dine with them on a regular basis. His late father, the Prince Consort, was good friends with the Alpha, so I imagine Oliver knows him better."

With a glance at the clock, she sighed. "I guess we should get going, we don't want to be late."

"Hold on, let me finish getting ready." While he had dressed in his shirt, jacket, kilt, and sporran, he still needed to put on his hose and shoes. Sitting at the edge of the bed, he pulled on his wool socks and garter flashes, carefully tucking in matching ribbons to hide them. Though it was an old tradition, putting away the decorative bit of the flashes signaled he was already taken. No one else here would know it, but it gave him a certain sense of satisfaction to do it anyway. After tucking in his *sgian dubh*—a small, decorative knife that was a family heirloom—he offered his arm to Julianna. "Shall we?"

They headed downstairs, where everyone was already assembled in the foyer, including—much to his consternation—Charity. His wolf growled, still furious at him for making their mate angry and jealous. Damn, he had hoped she wouldn't be here tonight, but as the Alpha's personal secretary, she probably stayed with him at Huntington Park when he resided here in the fall. And since Henry's wife had passed away some time ago, he probably took her as his date to many events.

When she tried to catch his eye, he quickly turned away. He was doing his damned best to show Julianna that the other woman meant absolutely nothing to him, and ignoring her to the point of pretending she wasn't even there seemed to placate his mate. However, if he knew Charity, she wasn't going to just stand by and allow the snub. He would have to be prepared, and if he had to, intervene before anything happened.

Ignoring Charity's dagger eyes, he headed for the empty space in the line between Reed and Oliver, but as he tried to tug Julianna along, a pinched-face woman with a clipboard came up to them.

"Ms. Anderson?"

A delicate dark brow rose. "Yes?"

"I'm Abigail Wentworth, His Grace's social secretary and protocol officer. Please come with me." She didn't give either of them a chance to protest as she dragged Julianna down the end of the line, right next to Charity.

Fuck me. If only he'd told the Alpha earlier who Julianna was so that she could be at his side where she belonged, not all the way at the end. But it was too late because the front door opened, and His Royal Highness, Prince Alexander George Arthur, Prince of Wales stepped inside.

Everyone stood at attention as Prince Alex made his way to them. Duncan had only seen him on TV and in newspapers, so it was surprising to see that he was much taller in person. From what Duncan had read, Prince Alex of Wales was in his mid-forties, married to his lovely princess who had already given him a gaggle of children. She was missing tonight, but he suspected it was because of their secret. After all, in the entire royal family, only the Queen and Prince Alex knew of the Lycans' existence.

The prince lingered as he chatted with Henry and Oliver, then he was introduced to Duncan, then to Reed and Elise. Next, stopped in front of Charity, who made a deep, formal curtsey. While it wasn't a requirement when meeting a royal, especially when in an informal gathering like this, he guessed Charity did it to either humiliate Julianna by making her look bad for not doing it or look foolish if she attempted it without any practice. Curtseying was an art, as he'd learned in all his time in England. *I'm going to wring her neck.* His wolf agreed.

He held his breath as Prince Alex stopped in front of Julianna, but to his surprise, she executed the perfect curtsey —a low, quick dip, keeping her eyes lowered until she got up. She looked magnificent, like she'd been practicing all her life. His heart burst with pride, and he wondered why he'd doubted her. She said something that he didn't quite catch, and much to his surprise, the Prince chatted quite animatedly with her for a few more minutes, before Henry came up to them and led the prince to the dining room.

Julianna looked at him, then winked. Beside her, Charity looked like she wanted to burst, and Duncan was glad that Abigail Wentworth whisked her aside before she could say or do anything to his mate.

"That was wonderful, darlin'," he said as came up to her to escort her inside the formal dining room. "I didn't realize Americans were taught how to curtsey."

Her mouth quirked. "Oh, you'd be surprised to know the things we're taught."

"What did you say to him?" he asked, not out of jealousy, but curiosity at her extended conversation with the prince. Aside from the Alpha, Prince Alex didn't say anything more than a few words to anyone else.

"I read online that he spent a year abroad in Italy when he was in college," she said. "So I told him that I was very happy to meet him, and I've been enjoying my time in his beautiful country. In Italian. My mother's family is Italian, and she insisted we speak it fluently."

"You did? What did he say?"

"He said thank you and that he was glad I liked England. And apologized that his Italian was rusty, because he hadn't had much practice. Then he asked me how I spoke the language and I told him about my mother and our restaurant." She picked off a piece of lint from his jacket. "So, needless to say, His Royal Highness has a standing invitation to Muccino's next time he's in New York."

"Clever girl." He snaked an arm around her waist and

pulled her to him, about to kiss her when someone clearing their throat interrupted him.

"Ahem." Abigail Wentworth's icy glare made them jump away from each other.

"Sorry," Duncan murmured as they walked past her and into the dining room.

The table had been elegantly set up with white flowers, linens, and the finest silver, as well as the Huntington china. Place cards had been set up to guide everyone to where they were supposed to sit, as was custom, but Duncan wished he could rip up the heavy card stock when he saw that Julianna was once again positioned far from him, at the end of the table on Oliver's left and across from Charity. It was a damn misogynistic tradition, treating untitled, unmarried women as the lowest ranking people in a group with royalty and peers, and right now, he hated it more than ever.

"So," Prince Alex began, "I've never met Lycans from any other country before."

"You haven't?" Reed asked.

"No, I'm afraid I didn't have the chance. The Royal Family has been an official Lycan Alliance family for over two hundred years, but we usually just know about the Alpha, his heir, plus the members who serve as our bodyguards."

"That's very interesting," Reed said. "I've heard the story of course, but I still find it ... impossible."

Prince Alex frowned. "Excuse me if I'm being rude, Mr. Wakefield, but the Alpha has told me that all his guests were from America, but you sound so English. Did you marry into the San Francisco Clan?"

As Reed began to tell his story, Duncan listened, really

listened this time. After what happened today at the statuary, he couldn't help but feel a nagging suspicion about the other man's story. There was just something about it ... he didn't know what, but there was something not right. Because he'd been distracted all afternoon, he didn't have time to ask Oliver about the statuary, but he made a mental note to ask him once they had a moment alone.

The dinner unfolded with all the pomp and ceremony befitting their royal guests, with white-gloved waiters serving course after course. He couldn't help but glance down the table at Julianna, who seemed to be holding her own, talking with Oliver and Elise, and ignoring Charity who sat across from her. Charity, on the other hand, kept glaring at Julianna. His entire body tensed and he had to rein his wolf in to stop it from growling at her.

"It is too bad that we've lost one of the good ones," Charity began as she put her napkin down on her lap after wiping her mouth with it. "Mr. Wakefield probably comes from good English Lycan stock, and it's such a travesty that his parents decided to migrate to North America." There was emphasis on the last word.

"England's loss is Canada's gain," Henry said graciously, raising a glass to Reed.

"I don't know how you coped with moving to America," Charity sniffed. "I mean, I know Canadians are a polite people, really, very English at heart. But across the border," she gave a delicate shrug. "Americans are extremely ... bois-terous, aren't they?"

Reed's lips thinned, while Elise looked shocked. Julianna, on the other hand, had a neutral expression, as if she didn't hear what Charity had said.

"Some might say that's an insult," Oliver said in a warning tone.

Charity laughed and waved her hand dismissively. "Insult? No, it was a little joke. Surely they can take a joke. Americans love to laugh. They laugh everywhere, all the time, even in the most inappropriate of times. I guess you can say"—her eyes darted at Julianna—"they're like the Italians of the Americas."

A dead silence hung over the table, and the air was thick with tension. Duncan would have given anything to be able to reach over and wring Charity's skinny neck.

"I think you've gone overboard, Charity," Oliver said.

She looked around, her lashes fluttering innocently. "Overboard? Why, Ms. Anderson hasn't said a word! Surely, if she thought she was being insulted, she would reply to defend the honor of her country."

And that's when Duncan realized Charity's tactic. If Julianna retaliated by insulting England, she would risk offending Prince Alex. But staying silent meant she would have to take Charity's abuse. Well, he wasn't going to sit down and let her do that to his mate. "Charity, you—"

"Oh, Charlene." Julianna looked up from her plate, her mismatched gaze flickering to Duncan briefly before turning to the other woman.

The other woman's nostrils flared. "It's Charity."

"Of course." Julianna's tone was similar to that of an adult talking to a small child. "Anyway, I'm not staying quiet because I agree with you."

"You're not?"

"Oh no." She put her fork and knife down gently, hardly

making a sound. "You see, I do *love* a battle of wits. But you appear unarmed."

Oliver burst out laughing, while Prince Alex very, unroyally, spit out the water he had just sipped. Henry, on the other hand, looked like he wanted to have a heart attack.

Charity's eyes narrowed into slits. "How dare—"

"Come now, Charlene," Julianna said dryly. "It was a little joke."

"I think it's time for drinks in the library," the Alpha declared. "Your Highness?"

When Duncan glanced over at Prince Alex as he stood up, he couldn't help but notice that the royal was having a hard time keeping a straight face, if the ticking muscle on the corner of his mouth was any indication.

As was dictated by protocol, the prince stepped out first, followed by the Alpha and Oliver. Duncan immediately walked over to Julianna to offer his hand to escort her. *Protocol be damned.* He wasn't going to leave Charity alone with Julianna, not when she was ready to swipe her claws at his mate.

He nipped at her ear as they walked out of the dining room. "You know, you're fucking hot when you put people in their place so efficiently. Hell, you're hot when you breathe."

She didn't say anything, but just gave him a mysterious smile, reminding him so much of that painting back home. It was fate, he decided, that brought that portrait to him and then later, its doppelgänger into his arms.

Drinks in the library were much more casual which he was glad for, except for the fact that it allowed Charity to take the empty armchair next to him and Julianna. Though he felt her tense, she said nothing and kept her face neutral, nodding and following the conversation with Prince Alex.

Half an hour later, the prince declared it was time to go. "Thank you so much for a lovely evening." As he stood up, everyone else did as well. "I'm sorry to cut it short, but I must head to one more event before I retire for the evening."

"You honor us with your presence," Henry said with a bow.

"No, it really was a nice way to break up the usual boring royal routine. And"—he smiled at their guests and winked at Julianna—"it was such a fascinating evening with fascinating people."

The prince bid his final goodbyes, and the Alpha walked out of the room with him.

"Wow," Elise declared when they all sat back down. "That was something."

"Dining with a royal." Reed shook his head. "Not even when I was—I mean, I never thought I would ever experience something like that."

"Well, not all royals are stuffy and boring," Charity declared. "Oh, Duncan, don't you have a friend who's a prince of some little country out East?"

"Karim, right?" Oliver offered. "The Prince of Zhobghadi."

"Yes." Duncan nodded at Oliver. "We went to Eton together, a year behind you."

"Awfully large fellow," Oliver said. "But very quiet and polite."

"He's always in the papers. Oh, his mother was English, right?" Charity bobbed her head at Duncan. She leaned forward, her voice lowering. "You know what they said about her."

Deep anger sliced through him at the mention of the gossip and his body tensed as he trained his eyes on her, wishing to God his gaze could cut her in two.

Charity, however, seemed glad she finally got his attention and continued. "They say she was—"

"Does your ass ever get jealous of the shit that comes out of your mouth, Charlene?" Julianna gripped his hand tight.

Charity's face flashed anger for a brief second, but she quickly recovered. "Oh Duncan, do you remember that dinner we had at that lovely French place on Bond Street? We shared the best chocolate soufflé."

"And they had that terribly snooty waiter," Oliver added as he looked meaningfully at Julianna. Duncan sent a silent thanks to his friend.

Charity didn't seem thwarted. "I do miss exploring those little cafes and bars with you whenever you would stay in London for your short breaks. Of course, these days, I don't have much time, but I'd love to go back to the Indian place where we—"

"Oh my God, woman, have you no pride?" Julianna loudly slapped a hand on her forehead. "I feel so mortified for you right now."

Charity let out an indignant and undignified yelp. "Mortified for me? You've got to be joking. You think you can keep him? I'd like to see you try."

"And I'd like a unicorn." Julianna's tone was pure amusement. "But we can't always have what we want, can we, Charlene?"

"For the last time, it's Cha—" She stopped, her eyes

flashing with anger. Then, the corner of one lip curled up into a cruel smile. "I had him first."

"Congrats," Julianna replied without missing a beat. "Did you want a cookie?" Charity's face turned a violent shade of purple, but before she could say anything, Julianna put a hand up. "And FYI, *Charity*: lying to get a man to fuck you doesn't count."

"You cunt whore!" Charity shot to her feet. "I'm going to—"

"You'll not be doing anything," Duncan snarled as he stood up, towering over Charity. "I'll not stand by while you insult my True Mate."

All the color drained from Charity's face. "Your ... True Mate?"

"Yes. Julianna is my True Mate, and any insult to her is an insult to me." He took a menacing step forward. No, he wasn't going to hurt her—he didn't do that to women, no matter how mad he was—but he was hoping to get the point across that Julianna was his, and no one was going to get away with disrespecting her. "We'll move to a hotel tonight. I'll not stay under the same roof with someone as vile as you."

"I couldn't agree more." All eyes turned to the door, where Henry was standing, his hands fisted at his side and jaw tense. "But please, Duncan, stay. Ms. Pitt-Lane, please pack your things and leave. I'll have your car brought around."

"B-b-but, Alpha—"

"Now." Pure power emanated from the Alpha, making it difficult to breathe. "And we'll discuss the future of your employment on Monday."

Charity's face fell and her eyes dropped to the floor. "Y-yes, Alpha." She turned toward the door and marched out.

The Alpha walked toward Duncan and Julianna. "Duncan, Julianna, please accept my sincerest apologies."

"You don't have to apologize for her, Alpha," Julianna said graciously. "That was not your fault."

"She said those things because she's a vile person," Duncan added.

"Still, her presence here is my fault." A slow smile spread across the older man's face. "True Mate, huh? Your father must be ecstatic."

Duncan chuckled. "Very much so." Beside him, Julianna had that mysterious smile again.

"Well, I think we've had enough excitement for the evening," Reed declared. "We should head up to bed soon, if that's all right."

Everyone agreed and finished off their drinks before heading upstairs. Before they separated, Reed pulled Julianna aside and said, "She would have been proud of you."

"Who?" Duncan asked.

"A mutual friend," Julianna quickly answered, then tugged at his arm. "Come on, I need to get out of this dress." She shifted uncomfortably, tugging the slit close.

"I need you out of that dress too," he said, wiggling an eyebrow at her. Not wanting to delay any further, he dragged her toward the direction of their room. As soon as the door closed behind them, Duncan let out a sigh of relief. "I hope you've forgiven me."

"Forgiven you?"

"Yes. For Charity."

"Oh, that?" She shrugged her shoulders. "Duncan, there's

nothing to forgive. Like I told her, lying to you doesn't count, and as for the others ..." She frowned. "We all have a past and have made bad decisions. It's part of who we are, right?"

He knew what she was trying to tell him, of course. And while the thought of Julianna having been with other men made him want to break things, he knew that was part of her past, and what made her who she was. His wonderful, beautiful, smart Julianna. "You were magnificent tonight."

"Really? Which part?"

"All of it." He stepped forward, crowding her so she had to move back. "When you charmed the prince. All your witty insults. This dress." His finger caressed the top edge of the silky fabric, and his knuckles brushed against her soft skin. "You were so regal, like a queen."

"Why, thank you. Oh!" She glanced around, probably just realizing that he'd walked her back all the way to the edge of the bed. "Duncan—"

"No more talking." He swiftly cut her off with a kiss before pushing her down on the mattress. Kneeling down, he lifted one long, slim leg and slung it over his shoulder. "It's time to lie back and think of England, my queen."

CHAPTER TWELVE

Julianna slipped from under Duncan's heavy arm and quietly crept out of bed. Not that she needed to be silent, because he slept like the dead. After brushing her teeth and doing her business in the bathroom, she put her robe on and headed to the small desk to sit in front of her laptop. With all the distractions of the last few days, she hadn't had time to properly answer emails and get some work done.

There were a dozen new emails in her inbox, but the very last one was what made her fingers hover over the trackpad reluctantly. It was from Lucas with the subject line *Next Steps*. She didn't have to open it to know what it was about. Lucas had her next assignments all lined up and was probably asking when to send the jet to pick her up.

If he had asked her two days ago, she would have said to get her out of there ASAP. But now ... Her chest tightened, and her wolf let out an unhappy yowl. The animal had grown too attached to Duncan.

Fuck.

She had grown too attached to Duncan. It was something she didn't want to happen, did everything in her power so it did not happen, but it happened anyway. Somehow, someway, that damned Scot had wormed his way under her skin. Last night, she didn't need him to defend her against Charity; indeed, she'd almost expected him to stay quiet so as not to offend the Alpha, but he stood behind her and supported her when she refused to take the other woman's rudeness.

Part of her sang with happiness. But then she remembered all the work she had to do and what was ahead. Lucas was counting on her. All the Lycans were counting on her, and now she was torn. Fate had barreled into her and knocked away all her plans.

She reached into her robe and lifted the gold disc into the palm of her hand. The wolf stared back at her forebodingly. *I can't let Lucas down.* This medal was a reminder that he trusted her and that she had so much more work to do in order to stop the mages.

"Haven't I exhausted you enough to knock that jet lag out?" came a sleepy, raspy voice from the bed.

She couldn't stop the smile forming even if she tried. "It's eight in the morning, Duncan. Most normal people are up at this hour."

"Aye, but we're far from normal." She heard him let out a grunt as he stretched. "Come back to bed darlin'. Oliver's going to be disappointed if we don't use up that box of condoms he gave me last night."

"You mean, the one you stole from his bathroom?"

"Potato, potatoh." The sheets rustled, followed by light footsteps as he came up behind her, so she closed the lid of her laptop. "What're you doin?"

"Catching up on emails. Don't you have work to do?"

"I haven't had a real vacation in five years." His talented fingers massaged her shoulders as he leaned down close. "My da and Finlay can spare me for another day or two. Speaking of vacation, maybe it's time you had some fun, too."

"This isn't exactly a vacation for me," she said. "I'm supposed to be working." That was something to she needed to tell herself, no matter how distracting Duncan was.

His mouth hovered over her ear; his breath hot. "Aye, but you've done so much already. Getting an alliance with two clans, plus the assistance of the royal family. That has to count for something, right?"

"I ... uh ... suppose." Damn him, it was hard to say no when he doing lovely things to her neck with his mouth. "What did you have in mind?"

"A day out in London," he murmured against her shoulder. "Just you and me."

Later—much later—that morning, Julianna found herself in the passenger seat of the sleek Aston Martin borrowed from the Alpha's fleet of cars as Duncan drove them into London. Seeing as he'd lived here for a few years, he already knew where to go to show her the highlights—London Bridge, Westminster Abbey, Buckingham Palace, Trafalgar Square, and Piccadilly Circus and—though Julianna thought it was terribly touristy—they also went on the London Eye.

"How about some food?" Duncan asked as they alighted from the glass cage.

"I'm famished," she declared. "But believe it or not, I'm getting tired of scones and pastries. I miss all the diverse food I can get in New York."

"I know just the place to go then."

They drove south, to a trendy little area called Brixton Market. He explained that this was the center of the Afro-Caribbean community in London. They popped into a Turkish cafe and feasted on meat skewers and flat bread. Afterwards, they walked down the rows of shops marveling at the colorful handicrafts, fabrics, bric-a-brac, and exotic spices all around them.

She dragged him from shop to shop, and while he didn't seem to mind, she could tell he was getting impatient. "One more store, I promise." While she wasn't a fan of shopping, she realized she hadn't gotten anyone any souvenirs from her trip. She had seen the cutest baby onesies in one of the shops, and she wanted to go back to get matching ones for her future nieces or nephews. "Oooh!" She held up little socks in a blue color. "Aren't these adorable?"

"You'd prefer a boy, huh?" Duncan wiggled his eyebrows. "I'd be happy with either, as long as our baby was healthy."

"Moron," she said playfully, swatting him on the face with the socks. A warm feeling spread in her belly at the thought of a tiny baby with dark blond hair and mismatched blue and green eyes.

He wrapped his arms around her and pulled her close. "Julianna, we need to talk—"

"Help, me please!"

The cry made them both stop. "What was that?" She glanced around. There was a woman frantically running in their direction, stopping to talk with one of the shopkeepers. He shook his head and her face twisted in agony as she turned away. When she locked eyes with Julianna, she sprinted toward them.

"Please, miss." Hands grabbed at Julianna's arms. "My baby. I can't find her." The woman's breath came in big heaving gasps. "I turned around for one second and then she was gone. You have to help—"

"Calm down, ma'am, I can't help if I don't understand you." Julianna placed her hands on the woman's shoulders to still her. "Breathe. That's it. Now, tell us what happened."

"My baby ... she's only two." Tears pooled in her eyes. "I told her to stay put, and she usually does. I handed my card over to the cashier, and when I looked down, she was gone!" A sob escaped her throat. "Please, you have to help me find her!"

"If she's only two, she can't have gone too far." She remembered her mother saying that toddlers did have a tendency to wander off. "I'm sure we can find her quickly. Where did you last see her?"

"Julianna," Duncan cleared his throat. "Maybe we should go to the information booth and ask them for help."

"Please," the woman cried. "The information counter is all the way at the other end. It'll take too long."

"Fine," Duncan relented. "Show us where you were when she wandered off."

They followed the woman as she zigzagged through the various alleys and lanes of the interconnected arcades. It was dizzying, with the riot of colors and smells of spices overloading her senses, but Julianna didn't want to waste any more time. There were so many places a small child could get into and lots of dangers abound.

"Where the bloody hell are we?" Duncan asked in an impatient voice.

"We—"

A wail sounded in the distance. "That's her!" the woman said. "My baby!" She darted into the nearest alleyway with Julianna and Duncan right behind her. The alley stunk, like rotting food and trash. The woman stood there, with her back to them.

"Did you find her? Is she here?" Julianna asked.

Slowly, the woman turned around. Her anxious expression was gone, now replaced with a menacing smile. "Stupid dogs. Can't believe you fell for that one."

Julianna's wolf's hackles rose, but before she could spring into action, her vision was filled with green fog. *Potion!*

She crumpled to the ground, and Duncan fell right beside her. This time, the potion felt stronger, as even her mind was shutting down. The last thing she remembered was three figures standing over them chanting strange words.

———

Slowly, Julianna regained consciousness, and while it took a while to get her wits about her, she instantly knew she was in big trouble, if the fact that she was lying on her stomach on a damp cement floor was any indication.

A groan beside her startled her. It was dark, but her eyes adjusted, and she saw Duncan was there too. Scratch that earlier thought, *they* were in big trouble.

"Duncan!" When she tried to move, she felt something wrapped around her tighten. "Fuck these fucking ropes!" She relaxed her body, and while the magical bindings stopped constricting her, they still kept her from struggling.

"Are you all right, darlin'?"

"I'm fine. I just feel like an idiot." Fucking mages. God, how could she have fallen for their tricks? Maybe it was the thought of babies and then seeing someone in distress that made her blind and naive.

"*Och*, don't be too hard on yourself, we were both duped." He groaned as he propped himself up against the wall. "Fine performance that lady gave. Shoulda won an award."

Well, no use crying over spilt milk. "We need to find a way to get out of here." Though it took her much effort, she managed to sit up.

"These fucking ropes ..." Duncan struggled, then let out a frustrated gasp. "How are we going to get these off?"

"Short answer, you *don't*."

A single bulb lit up above them, making her shut her eyes as the brightness overwhelmed her enhanced sight. Slowly, she opened her eyes. Her vision returned to normal, and the blurry figure in front of her came into focus.

Standing in front of them was the same mage who attacked them back in Scotland. He was wearing a red robe that matched the color of his eyes and made his pale skin look even sallower underneath the yellow light. "Amazing bit of magic, aren't they? Took a while to perfect them ... same for all our new tricks, really, but we've had three decades to plot our revenge."

"How many people did you have to kill and blessed witches to coerce?" she asked.

The mage laughed. "Does it matter? Magus Aurelius himself sacrificed hundreds of lives to ensure his legacy and power would live on." He leaned down to capture her chin in his bony fingers. "One more won't make a difference."

"You keep your hands to yourself, mage!" Duncan shouted. He tried to lunge toward the mage, but was quickly held back by the rope.

"Tsk, tsk, you dirty dogs really aren't too smart, are you?" Stained teeth bared in an evil grin. "Please, keep going. The more you move, the more the rope will squeeze every last bit of air from your lungs. It'll save me the trouble of killing you."

"No, stop! Don't hurt him!" The words came out of her mouth too fast, and she realized she had shown her cards too early. But she would do anything to save Duncan. "What do you want?"

"What else? I want the dagger."

"You already have the ability to teleport yourself and others," she pointed out. "That's how you were able to ambush us and escape, right? And how you got us here from Brixton?"

The mage laughed. "Smart girl. But that's only one piece of the puzzle. We need all three. Of course, with just the dagger, we may be able to change everything. But you already know that."

She swallowed, and a truly terrible feeling washed over her. *They couldn't possibly know—*

"So, why *else* do you think we want it?" He stared down at her with those scary crimson eyes. "No answer? Perhaps we should ask His Grace, Reed Townsend, Duke of Huntington."

Ice froze in every vein in her body. *They know.*

"Julianna?" Duncan looked at her, confused. "What are they saying?"

She swallowed and closed her eyes. He was never supposed to know. And even if he was, this wasn't how she wanted to tell him.

"I can see you're confused," the mage said. "We were too, until you and your companions came back from 1820 and proved that Hugh Richardson—or Malachi, as we now know —hadn't been lying in his diaries."

"Diaries?" Julianna asked.

"The day before he died—rather, before you and your companions killed him—he had his solicitor draw up an agreement with a large London law firm to act on his behalf in the event of his death. In the agreement, he stated that once a Ms. Elise Henney was born in the United States two hundred years into the future, that his diary was to be sent to one of three people." He took out a worn, leather-bound book from inside his robes. "Of course, in all that time, the law firm had gone through so many changes, and the agreement wasn't executed until an intern found the contract gathering dust in the archives and had it sent to me a few weeks ago. Too bad it came too late, really." He sighed. "We could have avoided all this, and you and your dreadful kind would now be our slaves."

"What's going on, Julianna?" Duncan's brows drew together. "I don't understand."

"Let me dumb this down for you, you sniveling dog," the mage said. "Julianna, Elise Henney, and that damned hybrid were transported back to England in the year 1820. Reed 'Wakefield' isn't who you think he is. He is Lord Reed Townsend, former Duke of Huntington, who traveled through time to wind up here in our present."

"England in 1820?" A cycle of emotions flashed across

his face—disbelief, confusion, hurt—before settling on one that made the pit in Julianna's stomach grow. Hurt. "You ... it *was* you ..."

"Ah, finally, you're getting it," the mage sneered. "Now, it's only a matter of time before we get our hands on the dagger and the last artifact as well. Daly left some clues as to where it could be, and soon we'll track it down, too."

Julianna ignored the pain in her chest. "You'll never get it! I'd rather you kill me first before they hand it over."

"Oh, you will die for sure," he said. "Both of you will."

No! Her wolf struggled inside her, yearning to be free. To kill the mage for daring to threaten their mate. "You monster!"

"Some might say you're the monster." His expression was chilly, making Julianna shudder. "You and your kind are abominations! The fact that you're still around makes me want to scream with the injustice of it all. When I am finished with you, there will be—" He stopped as the light-bulb above them began to flicker. "What's going on out there?" he barked.

The door flew open and someone—the woman who had tricked them—came inside. "I don't know! It's happening all over the building."

Realization flooded the mage's face. "It seems your idiot friends are mounting a rescue. No matter, we are prepared. At least the hybrid saved us the trouble of having to capture her and her mate." He turned toward the door, red robe sweeping the floor as he left the room.

The sound of the door slamming shut sounded so final in Julianna's ears. Fuck, this was a mess. The mages. The artifact. And then there was Duncan, who was still and silent as a rock beside her. Taking a deep breath, she turned to him. His face was inscrutable, but from the way his lips thinned and his jaw tensed, she knew he was not happy. "Duncan, I—"

"Julianna."

Every hair on her arm stood up as the familiar voice echoed in the dank, empty room. She double blinked at the person who had appeared out of thin air beside her. "C-C-Cross?"

The tall, Viking-like man nodded. With a wave of his hand, the ropes around her went limp and fell to the ground. "We don't have much time. Elise is distracting them —oomph!"

She didn't care if she hugged him too hard. Cross reminded her of home, plus it had been months since she'd seen him. She was overcome with emotion, and she had to find out if he was really here. And he was, if his solid bulk was any indication.

When he coughed discreetly, she let go of him. "But how did you know ... have you been here before?" Although Cross's power allowed him to move across great distances in the blink of an eye, it had one limitation—he had to have been there before or have seen it on a map.

"No. I tracked you down with the necklace. It's infused with my magic."

With a gasp, she placed her hand over her chest, feeling the gold disc under her shirt. "Holy shit."

The lights flickered again. "Like I said, we don't have much time." He grabbed her hand and reached out to

Duncan who looked like he wanted to protest, but it was too late.

A coldness wrapped around Julianna's body. It wasn't unpleasant nor unfamiliar, as she'd been transported by Cross a few times before. It was almost comforting in a way, reminding her of the past. Back when all she had to worry about was finding that dagger so she could get back home.

In an instant, she found herself back in Huntington Park's parlor. The room was empty save for herself and Duncan. He seemed discombobulated as his hands searched his own body.

"Don't worry," she said. "That feeling passes." She knew what it was like, the first time. She had been scared Cross might have left behind a vital organ. When she reached out to comfort him, he flinched away from her, and in that moment, it was like her heart ripped in two.

But there was no time to explain, as three more people materialized in the room. Cross, Elise, and Reed stood in front of them. "You're back!" Julianna exclaimed. "What happened?"

Cross rubbed his hands together. "I had to get Elise and Reed out of there. They were cornered, and we barely escaped the potion they threw at us."

"We need to go back and kill them," Duncan declared. "I'm not going to let them keep coming after me."

"I'm sorry," Cross said. "But they're gone by now. Disappeared."

"They can't just be gone!" Duncan growled. "Take me back there and I'll—"

"By now they will be. They've found a way to move

across short distances," Cross explained. "It's a difficult spell and requires three people, plus a lot of blood sacrifice."

Julianna's felt a chill at the last two words. The mages really were evil. "What happened? How did you find out we were kidnapped?"

"The mages sent a demand to Lucas to hand over the dagger in exchange for you," Cross began. "And then he called me. So, I came to Huntington Park to investigate, and sure enough, Elise and Reed confirmed you were gone and weren't answering your phone."

"Cross said he could track you with the necklace," Reed continued. "So, we found out where you were—a warehouse not too far from Brixton—and devised a plan for Elise and I to distract them whilst he rescued you two."

Julianna remembered the mage's words, how he knew about the dagger's time traveling properties. And it seemed, Duncan did too as he turned to Reed. "So, what was the purpose of you lying to us about who you were?"

"Excuse me?" Reed said.

"I know who you really are, *Your Grace*."

The entire room fell silent. Three pairs of eyes turned to Julianna. "You told him?" Reed's eyes burned at her accusingly.

"No," Duncan retorted. "I had to find out from *them*."

The tone in his voice made her throat tighten. "Daly ... he found a way to warn them." Hopefully that was enough explanation for now, because she feared if she said anything else, she would just break down.

"The mages know about time travel," Cross's eyes grew steely. "We must protect the dagger now more than ever."

"Duncan, you can't tell anyone," Reed pleaded. "Not your father. Not Henry."

Realization dawned on Duncan's face. "Wait. If you're ... if he's ... then you're also ..."

Reed scrubbed a hand down his face. "I know it seems impossible, but it's true. But—"

"No." He shook his head. "That's crazy." It seemed like it took much effort for him to look at Julianna, but when he did, his expression turned to anger. "All this time! You didn't say anything about the painting."

"Duncan, please—"

He pivoted on his heel and stormed out of the room. Julianna stood there for a moment, then ran after him, catching him in the hallway. "Please!" she reached out to touch him, but he flinched away again. "Duncan, listen to me—"

"You lied to me." He kept his back to her. "You didn't tell me. That was you in the painting, wasn't it?"

"I—yes." While she should have felt relief confessing the truth to him, it only sounded like the final nail driving into the coffin.

"Did you have any intention to tell me?"

What could she say? "No."

"No? You would have let me believe ... after I told you I would always tell you the truth." His arms were stiff at his side. "All this time, you were lying to me. And you were going to keep on lying to me."

What could she possibly say? He was right. She was a liar, and she knew all this time she was lying to him about the painting. A lie of omission, but a lie nonetheless. "I'm sorry."

He let out a huff. "I can't ... I don't know what to say."

Say you forgive me. "I ... I understand." Without saying another word, she pivoted on her heel and trudged back to the parlor. Cross, Reed, and Elise were quietly chatting, but they stopped as soon as she entered.

"Oh, Julianna." Elise came to her side and embraced her. "Is he still mad?"

It was too hard to speak. To breathe. So, she nodded.

"Don't worry, it's all a little misunderstanding. Once we explain, he'll come around."

"We could make him forget," Cross said.

"No!" Her throat burned as she spoke, and she couldn't stop the hot tears from trickling down her cheeks. "Don't, Cross. Please."

"There's ... a special potion that could make him forget specific things." Cross placed a hand on her shoulder. "It would erase certain memories, and he wouldn't remember the lie."

But I would. And she couldn't do that to him. Besides, Duncan's feelings on the matter were clear.

"We might not have a choice." He rubbed his thumb and forefinger on the bridge of his nose. "Just think of the repercussions of—"

"He's my True Mate." There it was, the admission coming from her own mouth. However, instead of the joy she should have felt, she only felt more miserable because she had driven him away.

Cross's entire body tensed, and the look on his face became inscrutable. Neither of them spoke for what seemed like an eternity until he said, "Then we will find another way."

Her body felt deflated, like a balloon, and a pain

squeezed her heart. "I don't want to be here, anymore." Surrounded by the memories, not of the past, but of Duncan. "Please, Cross, I want to go home."

"I'll tell the Alpha to send the jet."

"No." She gripped his shoulders and looked up into his stormy ocean-colored eyes. "Take me home. Now."

Cross looked confused, then gave her a curt nod. "As you wish."

CHAPTER THIRTEEN

DUNCAN WASN'T SURE IF THERE WAS ANY WORD TO describe what he was feeling right now. He only knew he wanted to destroy something or punch someone. Preferably that tall, handsome man whom Julianna had embraced so eagerly. So, that was *Cross*. It seemed irrational that he was feeling jealous right now, when his entire belief system was crumbling right in front of him.

He had always thought finding his mate would be simple, just like his parents' story. Find his True Mate. Fall in love. Get married. Have pups. The End. But no, his life had to have its own damned plot twists, and a damn big one to boot.

It didn't take a genius to figure out how all the pieces of the puzzle fit together. Indeed, he wouldn't have believed it if he didn't have the proof sitting in the library back in Caelkirk. No, the lady wasn't Julianna's ancestor or doppelgänger. It was Julianna herself. A painting from her time traveling adventures from 1820. The entire time, since she stepped foot in that library, she had been lying to him, and she had planned to continue lying to him, even after everything that had happened between them. Were his instincts wrong, too? Did his wolf recognize the wrong mate?

The animal growled, deep inside him. It didn't seem to understand what was happening, as it could only express rage because their mate was in distress, and he just let her walk away. He ignored it and headed back to his room—no, wait, all his things were in the room he had been sharing with Julianna. He cursed, then turned around and headed there.

When he entered, he realized he wasn't prepared for her delicious, honey sweet scent to hit him or the memories of what happened in that room. Despite what he was feeling, his body's instinct was to yearn for her.

"Duncan."

He froze at the sound of the masculine voice. "I don't really want to talk to you right now."

"Well, too bad."

"What? *Jaysus Christ!*" Reed pushed him inside and then shut the door. Rage burned through his veins. "Don't think I won't fight back, *Gramps.*"

Reed raised one aristocratic eyebrow and folded his arms across his chest. If it wasn't obvious before that he was raised to be a duke, it was now. "Actually, I'm your great-great-great-great—" His nose wrinkled. "I'm not sure how far along we are related."

This was madness. But the proof was right here. It was strange how Reed reminded him of the old London Alpha, with his dark ebony eyes. "But you're Oliver's *whatever-how-many-greats* uncle. The original Alpha who supposedly died."

"But I didn't die." Reed's voice was even and unwavering.

"They thought I did, but I was transported here a few months ago."

"Along with Julianna, right? Is she from back then?"

"No. Julianna was accidentally sent back, along with Cross and Elise. They sought me out because the dagger originally belonged to my family, and they needed to get back to this time. I recognized Elise as my True Mate, just as you did with Julianna. Did you feel it too? Like you were being ripped apart and put back together again?"

That was the closest thing he would use to describe the feeling, which only confirmed that Reed was related to his clan. "Aye. And the painting?"

"We didn't think we'd see it again." Reed ran his fingers through his dark hair. "It was an Italian painter who accompanied my grandmother. Signore Rossi. He wanted to paint Julianna. Look," he trained his ebony eyes back at Duncan. "We didn't mean to lie to you. To any of you. But what were we supposed to say? The Alphas of New York and San Francisco went to all this trouble to conceal my real identity. They feared that if the mages found out that I had traveled through time with the help of the dagger, they would try to use it to change the past."

"Fat lot that did you," he huffed. "They found out anyway."

Reed winced. "Yes. I apologize for whatever hurt you may be feeling. Julianna's not to blame though. It wasn't her secret to keep, nor did she want this burden in the first place. It was foisted on her unfairly."

His words hit Duncan like a speeding freight train. Perhaps he'd judged Julianna too quickly and harshly. Now that he'd had time to think about it and heard the explanation from Reed, he acknowledged the whole thing would have sounded absurd to hear the first time. If he put himself in her position, he would have had a hard time being honest too. "Fuck me. If Lachlan or Da were here, they'd call me a bloody *eejit*." He knocked himself on the forehead. "So, Uncle Reed, d'you know any good groveling techniques?"

"Er ..." Reed looked around sheepishly. "You should sit down, Duncan."

"Sit down?" A sense of dread crept up on him. "Why the fuck would I do that?"

"Julianna ... she's gone."

Gone? "To where?"

"Home."

"Then there's no time to waste!" He headed for the door, but a hand on his arm stopped him. "Great-whatever uncle or not, I'll deck you if I have to so I can stop her before she reaches the airport."

"No, Duncan, you don't understand." He let out a long sigh. "She's gone home. *Is* back home. In New York, as we speak."

He looked at Reed like he had been speaking gibberish. "What?"

"Cross took her home as soon as you left. With his, you know, magic."

"Motherfucker!" He really was going to kill that man. "I need to go then. To New York." But New York was a big city. How would he be able to find her? "You have to help me get to her so I can tell her that I'm sorry and I love her!" Bloody hell, he'd been keeping it inside all this time because he didn't want to scare her off, and now he hadn't even had a chance to tell her.

"Don't worry, Elise and I will do what we can. In fact, she was ready to come up here and thrash you if you didn't come around." Reed laughed. "And you promise not to tell Oliver and the Alpha?"

"I'll keep the secret to El Dorado, just as long as you help me get back to New York as soon as possible."

CHAPTER FOURTEEN

WHILE MOST WOMEN WOULD HAVE COPED WITH A broken heart by wallowing in bed and eating a fuck-ton of ice cream, Julianna was not most women. No, she planned to move on as quickly as possible, preferably, right this moment.

Cross literally brought her home to The Enclave, and after a quick shower in her apartment, she took a cab downtown to the Fenrir Corporation Headquarters on Madison Avenue. There was work to be done, though she was still planning to drown herself in a fuck-ton of chocolate chip cookie dough ice cream later tonight.

"Jared," she greeted the longtime Fenrir executive assistant as he sat at the desk outside Lucas's office. "Is my brother in?"

Though normally unflappable, Jared double blinked before his eyes widened. "Julianna? You're home! Are you all right? I heard about what happened."

"Hitched back with Cross." She tapped her foot impatiently. "Lucas ...?"

"You just missed him. He went downtown but will be

back in an hour. But he'll want to see you for sure. We were so worried about you, I'm glad to see you're all right."

"Thank you. I'm all good. Cross got to us in time." She really wanted to talk to Lucas and get her next assignment. Maybe he'd send her somewhere nice, like Hawaii, or Australia. "How about my Aunt Alynna?" As the head of the special investigations unit, Alynna Westbrook was technically her boss too, though she'd been reassigned to Jersey. She should report back to her and see if they needed her for anything.

"I'm afraid she's with Lucas."

"Hmmm." She couldn't just hang around here. It would drive her crazy sitting around waiting. "All right, I'll come back in an hour and try to catch Lucas then. Thanks, Jared."

Heading to the private elevators, she touched the biometric panel that allowed her to access the fifteenth floor, the secret level that served as the headquarters of the New York Lycan Security Force. Back when she first started, she had lived here for an entire year with the other trainees. The place was always buzzing with activity. Maybe she could find a recruit or two to spar with, just so she could expend the extra energy burning inside her. *Don't think of him.* But, dammit, telling herself not to think of him only made her think of him. And that was the reason why she kept on the move, not stopping the moment her feet landed in New York because she was afraid that when she did, she would start thinking of what happened, and the dam she had been building up to stop her emotions would just break.

Thankfully, the elevator's chime announcing its arrival on the fifteenth floor distracted her. She stepped out and headed to the training room. At this time of the day, they were probably doing drills or sparring.

Just as she guessed, the trainees were gathered on the mats, surrounding the two people sparring in the middle. Off to the side, she recognized two people—Nick Vrost, the current Beta of the New York clan, and his soon-to-be replacement and daughter-in-law, Astrid Jonasson-Vrost. Julianna winced as she came closer, noting that Astrid was heavily pregnant and looked like she was ready to pop. She raised her hand to catch their attention as she drew closer.

Nick acknowledged her with a nod, but quickly turned back to the fighters. Astrid, on the other hand, smiled brightly and waved her over.

"Hey, Julianna, I thought you were in Europe or something?"

"I caught a ride back with your brother."

Her nose wrinkled. "Cross was here? He didn't even say hi."

"Oh." *I guess Astrid and Nick didn't even know I'd been kidnapped by the mages.* It had all happened so fast. She could barely believe it was just hours ago she was just walking around Brixton, sharing a meal with—

Stop! Don't think of him.

"Julianna?" Astrid looked at her curiously. "You seem dazed. Anything the matter?"

"Er, jet lag." But her body was wound up. "I was hoping to do some sparring. It's been a while."

"I'd partner with you, but," she laughed as she looked down at her huge pregnant belly, "as you can see, I should have given birth yesterday."

"How much longer?"

"Doctor says two weeks, but maybe sooner."

As Astrid smiled and rubbed her protruding stomach, Julianna couldn't help the ache of longing within her. Her own wolf too, which had been silent until now, yowled pathetically.

No, she would not think about him or pine for him. Not when he was the one who shut her out and refused to let her explain. Unable to look at Astrid, she turned to the fighters on the mat.

Nick had moved away from the two women to observe the trainees at a closer range. The two men circled each other, neither making the first move. They seemed mismatched, as one of them topped the other by a good four inches. His opponent, however, was built like a brick wall, his broad chest and shoulders nearly twice the size of the other. Tattoos covered what was exposed of his enormous arms, and a dark brown beard covered most of his face, though the cocky grin he flashed his opponent was hard to miss.

"Is he from Jersey or New York?" She was pretty sure she'd remember a guy like that.

"Neither," Astrid answered. "Louisiana. He's a transfer."

"Transfer?" she echoed. The New York clan was one of the most difficult clans to transfer to, since everyone wanted to go there, and competition was tough. "Legacy, then?" A legacy transfer was someone whose parent or grandparent had been part of another clan and could then request a transfer back to the originating clan. Her Uncle Alex had been one.

"No." Astrid shook her head.

The tattooed transfer and his opponent finally grappled each other, and they fell to the ground. Julianna had to admit, he moved quick for a man his size. "How did he get into the training group this late in the year?"

Astrid lowered her voice. "Apparently Nick owes him a favor. He won't tell me what, but he cleared it with Lucas, who agreed."

"Must have been a huge favor." Still, how did Nick Vrost know this man? He was young enough to be his son. "What's his name?"

"Marc Delacroix."

As if on cue, he let out a growl and then rolled over his opponent, his bulging biceps flexing in effort.

"Hmm. They must grow 'em big down in the bayou," Astrid chuckled.

Delacroix now had the other man pinned to the ground and his arms locked backwards. His opponent yelped and tapped out, then Delacroix let go. The two stood up and shook hands. A few of the female recruits were definitely checking him out, and when he turned to them, he winked before grabbing a towel from a rack to wipe his sweat. As he was heading toward the females, Nick flashed him a warning look, which made him turn in the opposite direction. Still, there was a flash of promise in his eyes, and it was obvious this was a man who knew how devastatingly attractive he was.

"So, he's going to be part of the training team? And the Lycan Security Force eventually?"

"Maybe." Astrid turned to her. "Actually, Nick was thinking of foisting—er, switching him over to special investigations."

"Really?" Julianna snorted. "Mika'll shit a brick." Her cousin, and Aunt Alynna's oldest, was the second-incommand of the department, and though Aunt Alynna was years away from retiring, it was obvious her daughter would be the next department head. Mika did not like change and would surely resist the addition of someone new—and an outsider to boot.

"Since you'll be doing envoy stuff, I thought he'd be a good replacement for you. He's also got a set of skills which might be more suited to specialized work."

"Really? What kind of skills?"

But before Astrid could answer, Julianna felt a buzz in her pocket. Fishing her phone out, she checked the screen. "Lucas is back early and wants me up there. Anyway, good luck. With the baby I mean."

"Thanks. I'll see you around, Julianna."

She waved goodbye and headed back to the elevator and made a beeline for Lucas's office. Since he became CEO of Fenrir some months ago, her brother had moved into what used to be their father's office. It was pretty much the same, though she could see a few things had been upgraded like the large desk in the middle and the leather sofa seats in the corner where her brother sat. To her surprise, Lucas wasn't alone. His True Mate and wife, Sofia, was with him.

"Julianna!" Sofia shot up from the couch despite her advanced pregnancy. "When Jared told me you were home, I knew I had to see you." Her sister-in-law embraced her, and Julianna had to bite her lip to keep from bawling. She was home, finally, and for now, that seemed to fill the gaping hole in her chest she hadn't even acknowledged was there.

"I'm fine." Sofia finally let her go, though she was once again embraced, this time by her brother's strong arms. "Ugh, Lucas!" Though she protested, she couldn't help but find comfort in his scent—like the ocean spray tinged with sweet fried dough, bringing back memories of childhood at the shore with her family.

"You just about scared me half to death." Lucas took her hands in his and sat them down. "I might have threatened Cross to make sure you got home safe," he said sheepishly. "But I didn't mean it quite this literally. I could have sent the jet to pick you up."

"It's fine—I just wanted to come home right away."

"You poor thing." Sofia reached over and squeezed her on the shoulder. "Well, I, for one, am glad you're home now."

"What happened?" Lucas asked.

And so, she told them about what happened with the mages and what she had discovered about Daly, carefully omitting the part where Duncan was involved and knew about their time traveling adventures. *Cross said they could find a way.* Because if he didn't, Lucas may order him to erase Duncan's memories. Although it was tempting—to have Duncan forget that she had lied to him and everything could go back to normal—she couldn't do that to him. It just wasn't right.

A dark shadow seemed to cast over Lucas's face. "It's a good thing you got away and you're home. I'm about to make some changes, and while I won't make the formal announcement for another day or two, you should probably hear it first."

"What is it?"

"Papa, Daric, and I have decided to create a task force, whose sole purpose is to fight the mages. We're calling it the Guardian Initiative. For now, it will be loosely composed of people from the Special Investigations Division, Lone Wolf, and Sebastian Creed. As my envoy, you'll be part of this initiative, since you'll be traveling a lot on my behalf. Do you remember the necklace I gave you?"

She nodded, her hand immediately going to her chest where the medallion lay between her breasts.

"Everyone who is part of Guardian will have one. I didn't realize that Cross could use his own magic as a tracking device, but it'll come in handy if anyone's in trouble."

Straightening her shoulders, she strengthened her resolve and realized something. This is what she was meant to do. Who she was meant to be. "I'll do whatever you want, Lucas. Whatever you need. Tell me where you need me to go next."

Lucas chuckled. "Whoa, cowgirl. You were just kidnapped hours ago, then traveled across the world in the blink of an eye. I think you deserve a day off."

"What? No!" She didn't want a day off. Or any time off, or else—

"Julianna," Sofia began. "You promised you'd throw me a baby shower, right?"

"I did?"

"Yes, over video chat the other day. When I told you that Isabelle forgot to do it?"

"Oh right." She'd forgotten about that. "I mean, of course, I'll do it. Isabelle and I both will." It was her flighty sister's fault anyway that Sofia's shower hadn't been organized.

"Oh, that would be great." Sofia clapped her hands together. "Why don't we meet tomorrow at Petite Louve to discuss it?"

"I'll be there." At least she could put some of her frustration to good use by wrangling her wayward sister. "And so will Isabelle."

When Isabelle didn't pick up her numerous calls or answer the dozens of text messages she sent, Julianna decided it was time to hunt her down. However, her sister wasn't at any of her usual haunts; not Bergdorf Goodman's, Tiffany's on Fifth Avenue, The Plaza Hotel. Julianna even staked out Blood Moon until late evening. But still, there was no sign of her sister. She asked Astrid who was assigned to guard Isabelle, but when they checked, apparently, Isabelle had asked to stop her security detail some time ago, and no one had bothered to check if Lucas or Nick knew no one was watching out for her. "Apparently, she's not too popular with the bodyguards," Astrid had said. "She often used them to carry her stuff while she was shopping or close down entire stores so she wouldn't be disturbed."

It wasn't until the next morning that Isabelle finally picked up after what seemed like her hundredth call.

"Hello?" came the sleepy voice at the end.

"Isabelle? Where in God's name have you been? Never mind. It's eleven o'clock! Are you still asleep?"

There was a rustling of sheets, then a weak, "If you must know, Julianna, I'm not feeling well."

"*Pffft*. Well, go take a shower. Now. And then get dressed."

"I said I'm sick!" Isabelle said with a groan.

"I don't care if you have Ebola," she shouted into her phone. "You're going to get your butt over to Petite Louve by two p.m. and have tea with me and Sofia."

"Tea? Are you the effin' Queen of England or something?" Isabelle growled.

"Just do it. Or else"—she scrambled for something to blackmail her sister with, and the first thing that popped into her head was—"I'll tell Lucas and Papa that you haven't had a security detail in weeks. I bet they'd like to know where you've been going off to, all by yourself."

"What?" Isabelle sounded wide-awake. "No. Please. I ... fine. I'll be there." The line cut off.

That afternoon, Julianna arrived at two o'clock on the dot. She'd actually asked Sofia to come thirty minutes later so that she and Isabelle could have a chat.

Her wolf had been restless since she arrived in New York, and maybe she needed to let out some steam. Maybe it wasn't fair to Isabelle, but her self-centered sister had had it coming for a long time.

Isabelle arrived ten minutes late, and by the time she entered the nearly-empty restaurant, Julianna was rearing for a fight. "Look what the cat dragged in. Did you forget how to tell time?"

Her sister scowled at her. "I'm here, aren't I?"

"You know, if you spent less time preening in front of a mirror trying to take the perfect selfie, maybe you'd actually remember there are other people living in this world aside from you."

"Who the hell pissed in your cornflakes this morning, Julianna?" Isabelle spat. "Oh wait, you're always a bitch."

"Ha!" She leaned down and gave her a freezing stare. "That's rich, coming from a self-centered spoiled brat."

"Well, we can't all be perfect like you," Isabelle shot back. "And—" She slapped her hand over her mouth as her body tensed and her face went pale.

"Isabelle?" Julianna cocked her head. "Are you—"

But she didn't get to finish her sentence as Isabelle turned on her Louboutin heels and made a mad dash toward the bathroom. Julianna stood there for a moment, confused, then followed her into the bathroom. "Isabelle?" She winced when she heard the sounds of retching coming from the last stall.

When the door finally opened, Isabelle stepped out, looking pale as a ghost. She walked over to the sink to wash her mouth and her hands.

"Are you sick?" Julianna finally asked.

Slowly, she turned to her. "No." A single tear fell down her cheek. "Jules, I'm pregnant."

The single word—Isabelle's childhood nickname for her —shattered that deep anger she had felt earlier. Rushing forward she opened her arms when her sister fell forward. "Oh, Belle. Belle. Belle," she soothed, using her own child-hood moniker for Isabelle, as her body racked with sobs. "It's okay, it's okay. Belle, honey."

Minutes passed as they stayed like that, until Isabelle's sobs slowed to sniffs, and Julianna only let go when her sister did first. "Who's the father?"

Isabelle gulped hard. "It doesn't matter. He ... he left, and he's not coming back."

Outrage simmered inside her, and her wolf let out a guttural cry of fury. It wanted to hunt down this spineless bastard and make him pay. "*Prick*. Does this motherfucker know about the baby?"

She shook her head. "I didn't know I was pregnant until he left. We were seeing each other and then ... anyway it doesn't matter."

"Do you plan to keep it?"

Isabelle growled—really growled—and her eyes flashed

wolf.

"Whoa, calm down, she-wolf." She raised her hands in self-defense. "I wasn't implying you do anything drastic. You know I'll help and support you with whatever you decide."

Mismatched eyes rimmed with tears grew wide. "You will?"

"Of course. You're my sister, Belle. I love you."

"Oh, Jules." Isabelle began to bawl again. "I'm so sorry I called you a bitch."

"I deserved it." God, she wanted to kick herself for being so mean to Isabelle. And the truth was, she wasn't even mad at Isabelle—she was just the closest punching bag within reach. Her sister took the brunt of her frustration because Duncan dumped her and broke her heart. *Fuck.* She was in love with the bastard and still was. And he hated her guts.

"Julianna?"

"It's nothing." She swallowed, trying to ignore the emotions threatening to burst from her chest. *This was about Isabelle,* she reminded herself. "What do you plan to say to everyone? I mean, this isn't something you could just hide. It's going to be pretty obvious in a couple of months."

"I don't want to lie." Isabelle chewed on her lip. "And, well, there's one more complication. Something else that's going to be obvious in a few months."

"Huh?" When Isabelle raised her hand and drew a nail down her arm, Julianna panicked. "What the fuck! Isabelle, don't hurt—holy shit!"

Her soft skin split under the force of her nail. But the blood had barely trickled down her arm before the gash sealed right up, as if it hadn't even been there in the first place. "Isabelle ... the father is ..."

"Yes," she cried. "I didn't know at first, I swear ... I mean, I had a feeling but ... Jules, despite what people think of me, I'd never been with any man before him. It wasn't until after ... that I realized he was my True Mate. And no, I don't think he knows either."

Crap. This was getting more complicated. "What do you want to do?"

A sob broke from her throat. "Jules, will you be there with me when I tell Papa and Mama?"

"Of course." There was no question of that. "I'll be here for you throughout the whole thing."

"Thank you." Isabelle drew her in for another hug. "I just wish ... well, maybe if Mama and Papa had some good news after hearing about mine, maybe they won't stay mad for so long."

Julianna didn't know what to say, because she was pretty sure it didn't matter and their parents, particularly their father, would blow their tops either way. But, since she was trying to be a good sister, she said, "Sounds like a plan. Maybe we could think of something. Now, why don't you get cleaned up? Sofia'll be here any minute."

Isabelle winced. "I need to make it up to her for flaking on the baby shower plans."

"You will." She pointed to the sink. "Now, wash up and get pretty, okay?"

Isabelle splashed water on her face and reapplied her lipstick. "Do you really think everything will be okay?" she asked, her voice almost childlike.

"I have to be honest with you, I don't know what Papa will say."

"He'll be disappointed with me." Isabelle stopped, her eyes filling with tears.

With a sigh, she turned to her sister, placed her hands on her shoulders, and looked her square in the eye. "Yes." She didn't want to sugarcoat it for her, because Isabelle was going to have to grow up fast. "But he loves you."

"I'm not ready," Isabelle said unhappily. "I mean, I wanted kids, but in my mind, that was far from now. I don't even know how to change a diaper! I'm going to be a terrible mother, and I'll be all alone."

"No, you won't. I'll be here. We all will be. And the timing sucks." Isabelle huffed, but Julianna cupped her cheek. "Yes, the timing sucks. Especially with everything we have to worry about like the mages. But you can make it work. And anything can happen between now and that future you planned—what if there was no other chance?"

A sudden realization made her jolt, and that longing in her chest came back. There was no other chance. Not for her.

"I—" Isabelle's nose wrinkled. "Excuse me, we're trying to have a private moment here," she said to someone behind Julianna.

"Aye, I'm sorry, lassie, but I couldn't wait any longer."

Julianna's entire body froze. She was hallucinating. Yes, that was it. Wasn't that what women who pined for their exes did in movies? See them in every man on the street, hear their voices everywhere?

Slowly, deliberately, she turned her head. No, it wasn't a hallucination or wishful thinking on her part. Duncan stood there, in the flesh. His mouth turned up in a slight smile. Her wolf yipped with happiness.

"Hello, darlin'."

CHAPTER FIFTEEN

Traveling all day and night would have wiped anyone out, but seeing Julianna again made Duncan forget that he hadn't had any sleep in the last twenty-four hours. Those brilliant mismatched eyes were wide with surprise, and he was glad she wasn't tipped off that he had arrived because frankly, he didn't know what to expect once she saw him.

All the direct flights to New York had been sold out yesterday, and as it turned out, the fastest connection he could find was through Glasgow. He knew it was fate, so he asked his mother to meet him at the airport so she could bring him a couple of things. After his layover at Glasgow International Airport, he boarded his flight to New York and arrived at two o'clock in the afternoon, local time.

After slogging through immigration and traffic, he quickly checked into his hotel and waited for Elise to call him back to confirm where Julianna was. Elise had told him that she was at the restaurant, and it was just his luck that he had booked his hotel in the area, so he ran all the way here. He ignored the startled maître d', and when he didn't find her in the near-empty dining room, made his way to the facilities, hoping that he hadn't missed her or was at the wrong place.

And so, here he was, and here she was. His wolf howled —that's right, *howled*—with happiness now that it was near her again.

But what to say now? He'd thought of all the things he would say to her as he traveled over the last day, but for the life of him, he couldn't remember what those things were.

Julianna, on the other hand, hadn't spoken at all, though her mouth was open.

"Julianna? Who is this guy?"

Duncan turned his attention to the petite brunette, who, based on her mismatched eyes, was probably Julianna's sister. "Would you excuse us, miss? Julianna and I need to have a talk."

She looked at Julianna with an expression that said she wasn't leaving that easy. "Jules, do you know this man?"

Duncan lifted the large package he had propped up against the wall, then tore off the brown paper that covered the front.

She let out a gasp and pointed at the portrait. "Oh my God, Jules, that's you!"

Julianna blinked, seemingly snapped out of her trance. "Isabelle, honey, can you give us a moment?"

Isabelle looked from the painting, to Duncan, then back to Julianna. "I'll be in the dining room." And with a shake of her head, she left.

They stared at each other until Julianna spoke. "What are you doing here?"

He nodded at the painting. "I wanted to give this to you."

Her perfect mouth formed into an O as she stared at the portrait. "You came all the way here to ... bring me that?"

"I wasn't really sure why I brought it. It just felt right."

"Right?" she echoed, her eyes never leaving the painting.

"Yes. Julianna ..." He took a tentative step forward. "See, I don't deserve it. I don't deserve any part of you after the things I said." His breath hitched as her head snapped back and those luminous eyes stared up at him. "I couldn't bear to look at it anymore."

"Why ... not?"

"Because it would be a reminder that I had the best thing that ever happened to me in the palm of my hand and then I let it get away." His ground his teeth together. "No, wait. I didn't let you get away, I pushed you away. I'm sorry, Julianna. For what I said. Please, forgive me."

The air between them was thick with tension, but when her face broke into a teary smile, his heartbeat stopped for a second. "Duncan." His name on her lips never sounded sweeter and they both took one step toward each other, closing the distance between them that only moments ago had seemed as wide as the Atlantic. His arms came around her and pulled her into a tight embrace like he never wanted to let go. "Do you forgive me, darlin'?"

"I do," she said. "If you forgive me for lying to you."

With a sigh, he pressed his forehead to hers. "Reed explained everything, and I know why you did it. So there's no need to say sorry to me." And because he couldn't wait any longer, he kissed her, savoring the sweetness of her lips. He dragged his mouth lower, tracing down to her slim neck to bury his nose in her pulse so her sweet scent drowned him. "I love you, Julianna," he whispered.

"I love you back," she responded, and his heart felt like it would explode from emotion. He captured her mouth again, this time in a more sensuous kiss, his tongue dipping between her lips to taste her. Warm and willing, she responded perfectly, her mouth just as ravenous as his as if they'd been apart for years, not a day. She pushed her body up against his, and he let out a groan as his shaft rubbed against her stomach.

"Duncan," she gasped when she broke away. "I need you ... alone ... my place is so far away."

"Good thing my hotel's only a block away," he said, smiling against her mouth. "Let's go."

It was the longest five-minute walk of his life, but soon, they were alone in his hotel room. He practically carried her to the bed, their movements clumsy but quick as they removed all their clothing. God, she was beautiful and magnificent, lying back on the bed, her glorious hair spread around her, all smooth olive skin and sensuous eyes staring up at him. She was his. All his.

"Hold that thought, darlin'." He scrambled off the bed to dive toward his suitcase, throwing the top open to grab a foil packet, then marched back to bed. "I need you bad, Julianna," he growled. "I don't ever want to be away from you."

He crawled over to her, covering her body with his. However, before he could lean down to kiss her again, she wrapped her hand around his wrist.

"Wait."

He looked up at her, confused. "Is everything all right?"

She used her other hand to pluck the condom from his fingers. "I ... We don't need this."

His heart slammed into his rib cage, and it took him a second to recover. "Julianna? Are you sure?"

She nodded. "Duncan, you have it all. My mind, body, heart, and soul."

Dear Lord, he didn't think he could be happier or love this woman even more. "Aye, and as you do with me." He tossed the condom aside and then wiggled his eyebrows. "Now, let's make a baby."

Julianna barked out a laugh, which turned into a sensual moan as his mouth went straight down to where her shoulder met her neck and clamped his teeth down. He bit hard enough to mark her, but not to bleed, then suckled and licked at her skin. He knew she loved it, if the smell of her arousal mixed in with her sweet scent and her nails raking down his arms were any indication.

His cock was already hard, ready for her, but as he moved himself into position between her legs, the minx flipped him over so she straddled his hips. "Hey, no fair."

"Oh, this will make it fair," she purred, then slowly made her way down lower.

"Julianna, I—fuck!"

Her hand wrapped around him, and that sweet, sweet mouth wrapped around the tip of his cock. When he let out a pained groan, she popped him out from between her lips. "What? I thought you said you wanted to put my mouth to good use," she asked. "Should I stop?"

"Don't you dare."

She chuckled and bent her head down. Bloody hell, those plush lips of hers wrapped around his shaft was one of the most erotic things he'd ever seen. He shoved his fingers into her hair, giving it a soft tug that had her moaning on his cock.

"As much as I'm enjoying this, I can't wait anymore." He pulled her off him and then rolled her onto her back. She let out a squeak of surprise which was followed by a throaty moan when he rubbed the tip of his cock against her entrance. "Julianna ... open your eyes."

Thick, sooty lashes fluttered open, and her gaze struck something deep in him. It wasn't just the beauty of her eyes, but also what he saw in them—pure love. Even as he pushed inside her, he continued to look at her, hoping she too, saw the devotion in his eyes.

Jesus, being inside her without any barriers between them was like nothing he'd ever felt before. The need to claim her, mark her, breed her, was too overwhelming, but he also wanted to relish this moment. As if she sensed his need—or perhaps she felt it as strongly as he did—she pushed her hips up at him and squeezed him tight.

He let out a grunt and began to move, slowly at first, teasing her. But his minx didn't like that, and she scratched her nails down his arms and snapped her teeth at him. "Fuck me," she demanded.

"Ah, so impatient, my mate," he growled. He nipped at her neck, biting down hard enough to make her whimper. Then, he pulled his hips back and drove into her. Over and over again. Filling her to the hilt, each thrust making her cry out and run her nails down his back.

His eyes shut hard as he continued to pummel into her, feeling her body squirm underneath hers. God, he just wanted to feel her pleasure, so he could let go.

When her body quivered, and she clasped around his cock, he knew she was coming. Unable to hold back any longer, he let go, roaring as he filled her with his cum, his vision going completely white. His name on her lips as she screamed and her fingers digging into his scalp brought him back to earth, and he collapsed on top of her feeling the energy drain from his body.

Slowly, he opened his eyes, and his senses came back. The feel of her soft body under his. Her scent mixed with his. The lingering taste of her lips. And her soft sigh. Rolling over to his side, he slipped out of her to lay on his back, and she cuddled up to him, resting her cheek on his chest. His wolf let out a satisfied yowl.

Mate. Mine.

Moments passed in complete, satisfied silence. Finally, he spoke. "You changed your mind."

She planted a kiss on his shoulder, then looked up at him. "Yes."

"Why? I mean ... I'm just curious. I came here to ask you to give me a second chance, but I was also going to tell you I'm willing to wait for pups until you were ready."

"I know," she said. "This whole thing ... I always told myself it was bad timing. There's so much looming over us. But when else am I going to be ready? When the mages have been defeated? I can't let them dictate when I choose to be happy. What if there was no other chance? What if something happened to—"

"I'll never let anything happen to you." He silenced her protest with a kiss. "Or our baby." Jesus, a baby. Right now, she was pregnant with their pup. It both scared and elated him.

"I know." She chewed her lip. "I'm sorry, but I have to break my promise."

"Promise?" What was she talking about?

"About proposing marriage to men."

The words jolted him and he quickly sat up. "What the fuck? Who the hell are you proposin' to, woman?"

Her eyes sparkled as she let out a chuckle. "You, you moron. I think you should marry me."

It took a while for the words to sink in, and when they did, he burst out with laughter.

"Hey, that's not funny!" A pillow hit him in the face, and when she tried to scramble out of bed, he pinned her down. "I was joking, okay?" But the hurt in her face was obvious, so he kissed her long and deep.

"You misunderstood me, darlin'. Don't move, okay?" When she nodded, he quickly dashed out of bed, grabbed the second package his ma gave him at the airport and climbed back into bed. He held out the velvet box to her.

Cautiously, she took the box and opened it. "Oh. It's beautiful. Is it a family heirloom?"

Inside the box was an antique brooch, with two silver crowned hearts entwined. In between where they met was a large ruby. "Yes. It's called a Luckenbooth. In the old days, it was a betrothal gift."

"Oh." Her breath caught at the meaning.

"It's very old. Over two hundred years old. It's the same one Connor MacDougal gave Bridget when they were engaged." Elise and Reed had told him the entire story of what transpired during their time back in the 1800s, including how his ancestors had met. "I think she would have wanted you to have it."

"Duncan ..." She gulped hard as a tear slipped down a cheek. "Thank you."

"You beat me to it, but I'm still gettin' you a ring," he declared. "Well? Is that a yes?"

"Wait, who's asking who?" She let out a yelp when he tackled her and pinned her to the mattress. "Duncan, stop!"

"Ohh, ticklish, are we?" His fingers continued to torture her until she had tears in her eyes and was begging him to stop.

"Fine! Fine! Yes, I'll marry you." When he let go, she slapped his shoulder. "You oaf."

"I'm *your* oaf." He pushed her down again on the mattress and kissed her until she was breathless. Hell, he was gasping for air himself. "You've made me the happiest man alive."

"I suppose I'll get used to living in Scotland. And, well, I'm sure Lucas will find someone else to take over as envoy for me."

He detected a hint of sadness in her tone. "Darlin', you don't have to make that decision now."

"I don't?"

"No, of course not." He smoothed the hair away from her face. "Julianna, it's obvious to me that you love your work. You're suited to it. And you should do this work as long as you want and as long as you're able."

Her jaw dropped. "But ... what about the baby? And what about your work at the distillery? I'm not sure I can do long distance."

"Oh no, darlin'." The plan had already formed in his head the moment he left Scotland. It was another ace in his pocket, another thing he was planning to use in case Julianna didn't want to take him back. "I'm going with you. Wherever you go. I've asked permission from Da, and he agreed for me to take on the role of Caelkirk's envoy."

"What? But you're going to be Alpha and—"

"Not for a long time." At least he hoped not. Callum was still healthy and fit, and not even close to retiring as Alpha or president of Three Wolves. "I can still work remotely. He's actually asked me to travel more in order to promote the distillery abroad. And when it's time for the baby to be born, we can go home or come here to New York."

Her face lit up. "Duncan ... I don't know what to say ..." She lunged at him. "I love you."

Her plush body pressed to his made his cock stir. "And I love—"

The ringing of the telephone on the bedside interrupted him. "Who the fuck could that be?" No one knew he was staying here.

She frowned. "Aren't you going to answer it?"

With a deep sigh, he reached over and grabbed the receiver. "Hello?"

"Put my sister on the phone."

Duncan wanted to tell the man on the other end of the line to sod off, but that probably wasn't the best way to make a good impression with his future brother-in-law. So, he handed the phone to Julianna. "It's for you."

A puzzled look flashed on her face, but she took it anyway. "Who is this—oh." She winced and clamped her mouth shut. It sounded like she was getting an earful. "I'm sorry ... yes, I'm totally fine. Is she okay? I know I have a lot of explaining to do. How did you know ..." Her cheeks turned red. "You didn't have to ask him to do that. All right. All right. We're coming." She blew out a breath before handing him the phone.

"Is everything okay?" He put the receiver back.

"Yeah ... sorry about that. I, uh, kinda forgot my sister and sister-in-law were waiting for me at the restaurant when we made our escape through the backdoor. And when they couldn't find me, they panicked and called Lucas. So ... he had to call Cross to find me again."

"Find you?" *Wait* ... "Was that bastard in here? While we were—"

"No!" Her hands came to her chest, her fingers wrapping around the necklace she always wore. "He can track me with this and told Lucas where we were."

"Oh." Well, maybe the bastard escaped death for now. "What did he want?"

"He wants to see us now. He's at Muccino's."

"Oh."

"And my parents are there too. They just arrived from Italy. Apparently, they heard about what happened and they flew right back." A worried look crossed her face.

"What's wrong, darlin'? Did you not want me to meet them?"

"Huh? Oh no! It not that." She gave him a reassuring kiss. "I mean, it's all going so fast, but they'll be happy to know about you, but ... it's something else." She quickly told him about her sister, Isabelle, and her little predicament.

"That scabby bassa." He curled his hands into fists. "I'll pound his face in."

"You don't even know who he is or where he is."

"Well then, I'll hunt him down." His wolf, too, was eager to kill this unknown man. "She's my sister now, too, you know."

A great big smile spread across her face.

"And we'll support her, no matter what, you ken?" He kissed the top of her head. "Whatever she needs."

"Thank you." Her arms slipped around him, pulling him down for a slow, sensuous kiss.

"*Och*, darlin' ... if you're wanting to be outta bed soon, we should stop." His cock was already half hard again.

She made a sound of protest. "I suppose so. C'mon, it's time to face the music."

————

After getting dressed, they headed back to the same place where Duncan had followed her, however, they crossed the street to a different restaurant. The sign outside said "Muccino's" which, as Julianna had explained, was run by her mother's brother, while the Petite Louve was owned by his wife.

"Are you ready?" Her hand was already on the door, ready to open it.

"Aye." He wasn't sure what to expect from her family, but with the way they exited today, he could guess it wouldn't be a warm welcome.

The dining room was half-empty, but that was to be expected since it was not yet suppertime. Julianna acknowledged the young hostess at the station with a short nod and then led him across the room near the kitchens, and to a small door in the back. She opened it, and he followed her inside.

One wall of the room was entirely glass, showcasing the action in the kitchen. But that wasn't what caught his attention. It was the thick, tense air in the room, which only got heavier as all the occupants in the room turned to them.

"Hey, you're all here," Julianna said. "What's going ..." Her expression faltered and the young woman he had seen her with earlier—Isabelle—walked up to them. She and Julianna locked eyes. "You told them."

Isabelle nodded. "Yes."

"I said I would be here when you did."

"I know, Jules." She bit her lip. "But this was something I felt I had to do by myself. I can't forever depend on other people, you know. Besides, everyone was here, so I thought I'd save myself the trouble."

Julianna did a double take. "Oh."

"Yeah, Adrianna and Darius drove over as soon as they heard you were missing again. Er, sorry about that, by the way, but you just disappeared, and Sofia and I panicked. We thought he was a mage." She cocked her head at Duncan.

"He's not. He's my—"

When Julianna stopped suddenly, Isabelle reached out to hold her hand. "It's okay. I don't mind if you say it."

Julianna turned to Duncan, and he understood. She was worried because the bastard who impregnated her sister and then left her was her True Mate. He really was going to pound that man's face in—didn't he realize how precious it was to find the other half of your soul?

"Is Papa mad?" Julianna asked.

Isabelle shrugged. "See for yourself."

Duncan guessed the older man who was staring at them with intense green eyes was their father, *the* Grant Anderson, former Alpha of New York. It was obvious the man was on the edge, the worry lines on his face getting deeper with each second. "I'm sorry you had to face them alone, lassie."

She smiled weakly at him. "It had to happen. But I'm glad you two have better news."

Julianna tugged at his hand. "Our turn to run the gauntlet."

Duncan counted six other adults in the room, aside from the three of them. Julianna brought them in front of the oldest couple first. His wolf was wary, very much aware that it was in the presence of two powerful wolves. "Mama, Papa, I'd like you to meet Duncan MacDougal. He's my True Mate."

That seemed to stun them, and everyone else in the room. "True Mate?" The petite woman beside Grant Anderson gasped. From her dark hair and the mismatched eyes, he easily guessed this was Julianna's mother. "Oh my. That changes things."

"We thought you were a mage and kidnapped her." Grant Anderson's eyebrows drew together. "I'm not sure which I prefer right now."

"Grant!" His wife admonished with a chuckle. "Lovely to meet you, Duncan. I'm Frankie, and this is Julianna's father, Grant."

"Lovely to meet you, ma'am. Sir."

"Ohh, that accent!" Frankie tittered. "No wonder Julianna couldn't resist you."

Duncan was introduced to the rest of the family, including the current Alpha, Lucas Anderson, his Lupa, Sofia, and the Alpha of New Jersey, Adrianna Anderson and her mate and consort, Darius Corvinus. Based on the fact that the two ladies were obviously pregnant, he guessed they were all True Mates.

"The kitchen is preparing our dinner," Frankie declared. "Why don't we all sit down and I can grab us some wine—er, make that sparkling water."

"Wine, please," Grant and Lucas declared at the same time.

"I'll have the same, if you don't mind, Mrs. Anderson," he said.

"No problem." Her dazzling smiled reminded him of Julianna's. "And please, call me Frankie."

When she returned with the wine as well as some appetizers, the atmosphere was still tense. From the way the oldest Anderson and the youngest were seated at the opposite ends of the table and ignoring each other, it was obvious that despite how hard Frankie tried to include them both in the conversation, things were not going to get better. He could feel the tension coming from Julianna and her distress over the whole situation. Duncan decided to do something about it.

"You all probably don't know this, but I've been in love with Julianna since I was seven years old," he declared.

Forks and knives clattered on plates, and all eyes turned to them.

"What?"

"How the hell—"

"You can't be—"

Duncan raised his hand. "Aye, it's true. From the first moment I laid eyes on her portrait."

"The painting!" Isabelle cried as she shot up from her seat. "Hold on." She dashed out of the door and returned, said portrait in hand. "When you guys left, I took this with me. I figured you might want it back."

"*Madre de dio*," Adrianna Anderson declared. "That's you!"

Julianna rolled her eyes. "Thanks, Captain Obvious." Then she turned to Duncan. "Really?"

"Aye," he nodded reverently and began to tell them the story of how he first saw the painting and how it had come into his hands. Everyone listened with rapt attention, including his mate, since he had never told her the story either. "And then a few days ago, the real thing walks into my house, and I realize she's my True Mate."

"No way," Sofia said through a mouthful of pasta. "You can recognize your True Mate?"

"Yes, but Julianna didn't believe me," he said. "In fact, her first reaction was to punch me in the gut."

"Sounds like Julianna, all right," Isabelle said with a roll of her eyes.

"That's after I stomped on your foot because you wouldn't let me go," Julianna added.

"Oh, such a romantic story," Frankie said. "I'm sure your children will love to hear it someday. I mean ... you are ..."

They looked at each other and Julianna nodded, her eyes never straying from his.

"More grandchildren for us, then." Frankie looked up at her husband, whose expression had softened.

"Every one of them a welcome blessing," Grant Anderson declared. Though he wasn't looking at anyone in particular except his wife, the thick tension in the room had lessened.

Frankie had tears in her eyes which she quickly wiped away. "I have to warn you," she said to Duncan. "Twins run in my family."

"In his too," Julianna said with a sigh.

"No, they don't."

Julianna's brows snapped together. "I saw Finlay and Fraser with my own eyes."

Duncan could barely suppress the laugh bubbling in his chest. "They're not twins—"

"Well, they sure did look identical to me."

"—they're *triplets*."

A shocked silence hung in the air.

"Trip ... lets?" Julianna choked.

"Yes. Fletcher lives abroad, so you haven't met him."

Everyone at the table looked at them, and the silence was broken by Isabelle Anderson's rich laugh. "Oh. My. *God*. Triplets!"

"That's not funny, Isabelle!" Julianna fumed.

"Yes, it is! Good Lord, talk about karma. *Oww!*" Isabelle cried. "Did you really have to hit me with your breadstick?"

"Stop it, you two," Grant Anderson warned.

"She started it!" Isabelle and Julianna chorused.

"*Ay basta*, stop!" Frankie got up from her chair. "Duncan will think I've raised you in a barn! Now, pipe down or no dessert."

Julianna and Isabelle shirked back. Duncan was glad because he really was looking forward to the tiramisu Frankie had promised. And from then on, the atmosphere in the room lightened considerably.

Julianna leaned her head toward him and slipped her hand into his to give it a squeeze. "Thank you," she whispered. "For everything."

He gave her a quick kiss on the nose. "Anything for you, darlin'."

EPILOGUE

A FEW DAYS LATER, JULIANNA AND DUNCAN WERE AT the Fenrir Corporation headquarters on their way to the top floor for the first official meeting of the Guardian Initiative. They'd told Lucas about Duncan's new role as Caelkirk's envoy, and so he was invited to join them.

They took the private elevators to the executive floor, and as the doors opened, Duncan smiled at her impishly. "What? See, I told you we wouldn't be late."

"Yeah, that's because I told the Uber driver I'd give him an extra ten bucks to run that red light."

"*Och*, as I recall, you were screamin' like a banshee, pullin' at my hair while I was between your legs—"

"Shush." She glanced around, and let out a relieved breath when she saw there was no one there except Jared, who was sitting just outside of Lucas's office. "Are we late?"

"Just in time, but you're the last ones." He opened the door. "Go right ahead."

They rushed inside, where a small group of people were

gathered around Lucas's desk. Her brother raised a brow at them. "Finally, we're all here."

"Sorry ... er, the Uber took a while," she said as they sat on the last two empty chairs. She recognized almost everyone in the room, so it was only for Duncan's benefit that Lucas made the introductions.

"Everyone," Lucas began. "This is Duncan MacDougal, heir apparent to the Alpha of Caelkirk of Scotland, and also his envoy. I've invited him to join the Guardian Initiative, and he's accepted. Duncan, you already know my mother and father. This," he nodded to the older, blond man on his left, "is Daric Jonasson. He's been a part of our clan for almost thirty years, and you've probably met his son, Cross."

Duncan tensed beside her, but she put a hand over his. "I've met him," he said.

Julianna rolled her eyes. She couldn't believe he was still sore about the whole Cross thing, but she supposed it was understandable, given how extra protective he was of her these days.

"This," he indicated the young woman next to Daric, "is Mika Westbrooke, our cousin. She's assistant director of the Special Investigations Division, and she and Daric will lead the team." Mika nodded at Duncan and smiled at Julianna. While they weren't particularly close while growing up, she got to know her cousin a lot as they worked together. She was smart, capable, and strong, and Julianna often joked she wanted to be like Mika when she grew up. And certainly, after overcoming the tragedy that happened to her a while back, Julianna's respect for Mika grew tenfold.

"Also on our team are representatives from Lone Wolf Investigations. That's Killian Jones, current director"—Lucas nodded to the older man with silver streaks in his dark hair —"And their junior associates, Arch Jones and Lizzie Martin." The younger man was obviously Killian's son, as he looked exactly like his father, save for the violet eyes. Lizzie she remembered, as she was her cousin Hannah's sister-in-law. In the austere offices, she looked out of place with her neon-pink shirt, leather skirt and thigh-high boots, her strawberry blonde hair pulled up in pigtails. She popped the lollipop she was sucking on out of her mouth and waved at them.

"Finally, we also have Sebastian Creed and his son, Wyatt."

Julianna felt her wolf shrink back warily, and Duncan sat up a little straighter in his chair. It wasn't a surprise seeing as they were in this enclosed space with the world's only dragon shifter. When she was much younger, all the kids in the clan had loved seeing Sebastian Creed transform into his gigantic, hundred-feet tall gold dragon. He would even give them rides. However, it seemed as they grew older and their wolves appeared, so did that sense of self-preservation. Though Sebastian was very much in control of his animal, she still felt apprehensive around him as her wolf recognized the predator in him that was very much at the top of the food chain.

"Lord Warwick," the younger Creed said to Duncan.

Duncan's brows knitted together. "I'm sorry, have we met before?"

Wyatt Creed was just as large and handsome as his father, but his eyes were such a light hazel that they were almost yellow. "I was in the same year at Eton as your brothers," he explained. "We were introduced once. Baroness Oxley is my grandmother."

His tone was posh, and there was something about his air that rubbed Julianna the wrong way. It was like he thought himself better than anyone else in the room.

"Oh. Er, nice to meet you again. And please, just call me Duncan."

"Now that everyone is here, I think we can begin," Lucas said. "As you know, although the mages have been quiet again for the last couple of months, there have been two more attacks in the last weeks where they targeted Julianna, as well as Elise and Reed Wakefield." He looked at Daric and Grant, who both nodded. "There's something I need to share with the task force, something we've been trying to keep under wraps. However, it seems the mages have found out anyway, which is why I'll tell you about it now. But we do ask that we keep this within this room, if possible. You see—"

A loud ringing pierced the air, making everyone reach for their pockets or purses.

Sebastian Creed stood up. "Sorry, that's me ... and ..." He glanced at the screen. "Apologies, this is urgent. Please, go on." He stepped to the side, cupping his hand over the phone as he spoke.

"As I was saying," Lucas continued. "The dagger we have in our hands is capable of some truly powerful magic. It can allow for—"

Lucas was interrupted by an almost inhuman growl from Sebastian Creed. "*WHAT THE FUCK*?"

The air in the room suddenly became thick, and Julianna reached for Duncan's hand as her wolf became agitated. Looking around at the other Lycans, it was obvious everyone could feel the rage burning from Sebastian. His hulking form was stretched to full height as he shouted into the phone.

"What do you mean you *lost* her? There's nothing out there ... sandstorms? I don't give a fuck about sandstorms! With the money I'm paying you, you should have followed her to *hell*. I'm going to rip your head off and then I'm going to...."

Julianna winced as Sebastian described in graphic detail what he was going to do to the caller's head. Around them, everyone was eerily quiet and still as if afraid to say a word or break the tension in the air. Even the usually cool and collected Lucas looked unsure. Wyatt, however, stood up and walked over to his father.

"Where were you when she disappeared?" Sebastian turned to face them as his son put a hand on his shoulder. "The border of ..." The atmosphere grew so thick it was hard to breathe.

Julianna thought for sure she was seeing things, but from the way Duncan shot up from his seat and placed his body between her and Sebastian, she knew it did happen. The man's slate-colored eyes turned a brilliant gold, just like the color of his dragon scales.

"Sebastian." Daric came close to him. "Calm yourself or I shall have to knock you out with a potion."

His head snapped to the warlock. "Calm myself? How the hell can I?" he roared. "She's gone. My daughter is fucking *gone*, despite all the goddamn people—idiots—I hired to watch her! What if it was Astrid?"

"We will find her," Daric assured him.

"She's one of us," Lucas added. "Now, tell us what happened."

Sebastian seemed to calm enough to sit down, and he began to talk.

"*Jaysus, Mary, and Joseph,*" Duncan whispered. "Are things always this exciting around here?"

"Not usually." But what could have made Sebastian nearly release his dragon? "Are you regretting joining this circus?"

He laughed. "No way. I almost saw a dragon."

She looked warily at Sebastian, who seemed agitated again. "You must have a death wish, you crazy man."

"*Och*, crazy, yes, but only for you."

Despite the big storm brewing ahead, Julianna was glad that Duncan was by her side. Though it was only a while ago she wanted to get away from the crazy Scot, now she couldn't wait to spend the rest of her life with him.

Not quite The End ...

————

A few days ago...

Desiree Desmond Creed, Deedee to her friends, placed her hands on her hips. *I never thought I'd be in a mess like this, but here I am.*

And how did she end up here? Well, as it did with most stories, this one started with a boy.

Er, man, really.

But she had known Cross Alexander Jonasson since he was a boy, and she was a girl. Indeed, their mothers were best friends and they were born months apart. They grew up together. Playmates. Neighbors. Best friends, along with his sister, Astrid.

And when she was of that age when girls started to notice boys, she noticed *Cross*.

How handsome he was.

How tall he was—which was rare especially after her unfortunate six-inch growth spurt at fourteen.

And how nice he was to her. He knew everything about her and she knew everything about him.

At least she thought she did.

So, after years of unrequited pining, she had hoped to make it ... well, requited.

But as it turned out, it wasn't.

In a fit of passion—or perhaps, the thought of the end of the world coming—she confessed her feelings to him. Which turned out to be unequivocally *un*requited.

"I'm sorry, Dee. I love you, but only as a friend."

And so, with her heart trampled, she did the only logical thing: run away halfway across the world.

Which is how she ended up lost in the desert, somewhere in between the border of Afghanistan and Pakistan, in the midst of an impending sandstorm.

———

Ready for the next book?
Daughter of the Dragon is out now!
At your favorite online bookstores.

Thank you for reading Julianna and Duncan's story and coming with me on this journey.

I have some extra HOT bonus scenes for you - just join my newsletter here to get access:

http://aliciamontgomeryauthor.com/mailing-list/

You'll get access to ALL the bonus materials from all my books and my **FREE** novella **The Last Blackstone Dragon.**

ABOUT THE AUTHOR

Alicia Montgomery has always dreamed of becoming a romance novel writer. She started writing down her stories in now long-forgotten diaries and notebooks, never thinking that her dream would come true. After taking the well-worn path to a stable career, she is now plunging into the world of self-publishing.

facebook.com/aliciamontgomeryauthor

twitter.com/amontromance

bookbub.com/authors/alicia-montgomery

Made in the USA
Las Vegas, NV
27 November 2023

81685498R00152